WINTERFELL

Tania,

It is a pleasure working with you and I am blessed to call you friend!

Enjoy the Read

Hedun-Powidajko

WINTERFELL

A novel

By

Linda Fedun

Copyright © 2009 by Linda Fedun.

Library of Congress Control Number: 2010916365
ISBN: Hardcover 978-1-4568-0936-2
Softcover 978-1-4568-0935-5
Ebook 978-1-4568-0937-9

All rights reserved. No part of this book may be reproduced or transmitted in any form or by any means, electronic or mechanical, including photocopying, recording, or by any information storage and retrieval system, without permission in writing from the copyright owner.

This is a work of fiction. Names, characters, places and incidents either are the product of the author's imagination or are used fictitiously, and any resemblance to any actual persons, living or dead, events, or locales is entirely coincidental.

This book was printed in the United States of America.

To order additional copies of this book, contact:
Xlibris Corporation
1-888-795-4274
www.Xlibris.com
Orders@Xlibris.com

Dedication

This book is dedicated, with love, to my two favorite Williams:
For William Andrew Beggs
Born in 2009
I wrote this book waiting for his arrival.
and
My late father, William (Bill) Fedun
1926-2005

Acknowledgements

I have to thank all the people who came along with me on this journey. Many individuals have come into my life to inspire, influence and support me in many of my endeavors.
My son, Elliot Powidajko, and my daughter, Kasey Beggs, are always there for me. They are my joy and my reason for life.
My parents, Jennie and Bill Fedun, have been both my most trusted supporters and motivators throughout my life.
My uncle, Dr. Graham Hughes, lovingly and expertly worked untold hours to read and re-read to help me edit my novel.
My friends, my colleagues, and my students read my novel and encouraged me with their comments.
My grade 8 student, Andrew Kanas who dared me to read the genre of Fantasy
all those years ago.
Everyone who kept telling me that I could do it!

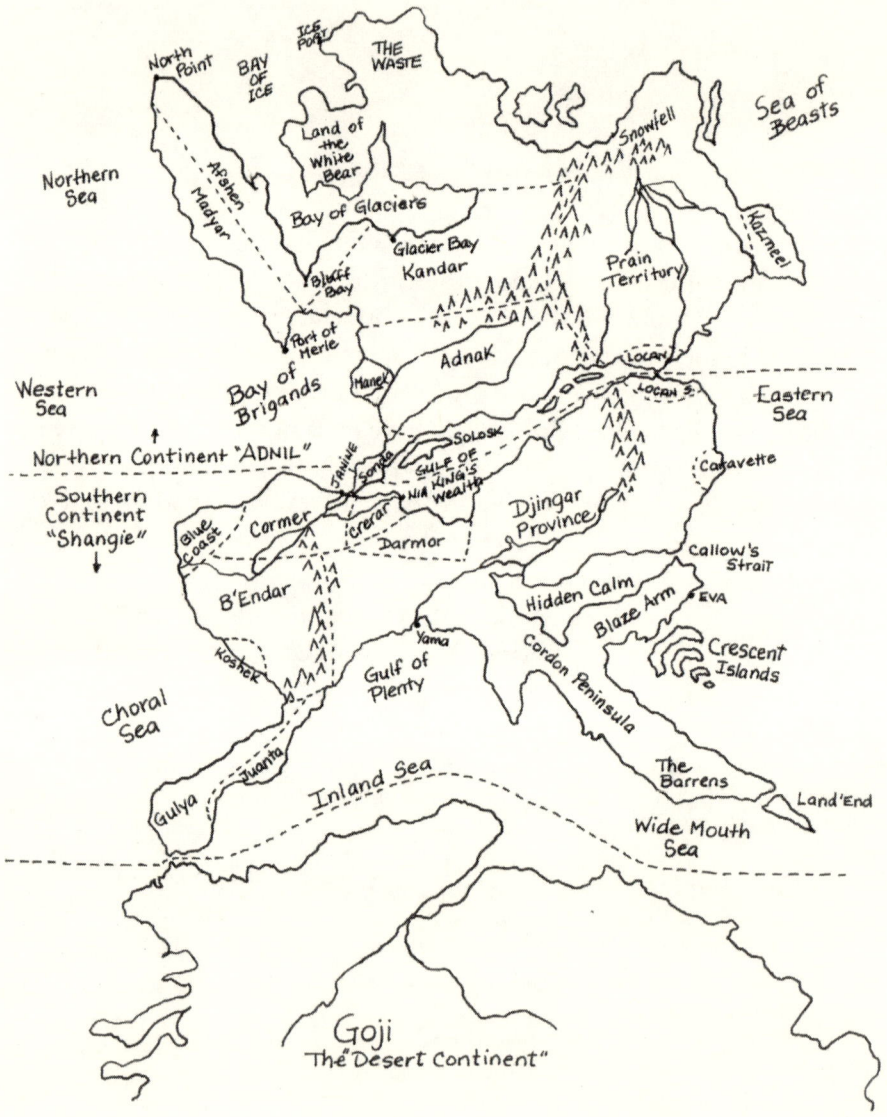

CHAPTER 1

FIONA AND LARS loved their twins dearly but they were not their biological parents. The babies arrived one day, delivered by an illiterate, old and decrepit woman who was almost blind and completely mute. Her disability made it impossible for her to tell the parents anything except for what was scratched on a small rolled parchment which she handed to them. The hag just walked off once she knew that the babies would be taken care of. Their adoptive parents named then Den and Fannie as instructed by the mysterious parchment and they showered them with unconditional love. Even as infants, Den and Fannie were never content unless they were in physical contact with each other. They were happy together and when they cried it was always at the same time. Their moods and thoughts seemed to project from one infant to the other. They grew into strikingly beautiful toddlers who were never seen apart from each other. Two little heads of tightly wound black curls could always be seen following their mother wherever she went. With very little reason to speak, they seemed like very well behaved and introspective children. No one suspected that the children were engaged in constant communion with each other.

When Den and Fannie were only three years of age, a fire erupted in the hut where the blacksmith plied his craft. It quickly spread to the neighbouring stable where the horses began to scream in panic. With two toddlers on her hips, Fiona, the children's adoptive mother, rushed to lend assistance. When the blaze came into their field of vision and they could hear and feel the panic of the horses, the children became unnerved. As suddenly as it had started, the fire ceased to exist. The damage was apparent but the horses were saved and the fire was completely snuffed out. All those who had witnessed the bizarre occurrence were stymied. No one had ever known a fire to just stop burning. One moment it was raging and out of control and in an instant it was simply snuffed out of existence. Small wisps of smoke were all that was left of the inferno.

When the children were five years old, a strange affliction began to cause all the cows in the village to grow weak and to stop producing milk. Den and

Fannie both had a special connection to all the animals they encountered so that they could sense and even experience their suffering. Their concern and empathy somehow caused the animals to recover from this blight that threatened to leave the village without a single cow. Not until several other unexplained incidents took place did the villagers begin to suspect the children's connection.

Gossip quickly spread and was embellished with each retelling. Even though the children only seemed to perform their magic for the common good, superstition abounded and made people afraid of that which they did not understand. If the children had the power to control fire and heal sickly cows, who knew what they could be capable of if they became angered?

This was the beginning of the time that Lars and Fiona began to constantly move their small family from one village to another. They never stayed in one place longer than six months and they often stayed for less time than that. It was very difficult to establish oneself in a new community and living the life of transients was becoming very wearing on Lars and Fiona. They both longed to live in a town or village where they could build a house, grow a garden, raise some farm animals and have friends with whom to live their lives in a normal fashion.

The year in which Den and Fannie turned nine, Lars and Fiona finally found themselves at their wits' end. The last six years had been a whirlwind of moving and meeting new people. They had not been able to establish themselves in a community where they could live peacefully and productively.

Fiona was a midwife whose skills were always in demand and Lars was an excellent farmer. His plantings never failed to produce healthy and nutritious vegetables and fruits. It was less than a year since they had transplanted their family to the outskirts of the Town of Nia, located south of the Moran River, not far from the coast of the Gulf of the King's Wealth. Thus far, they had been accepted as hardworking, honest individuals who worked toward the betterment of the community.

The soil in Crerar was fertile and the river which ran along the northern perimeter of the property where Lars built a makeshift home provided the irrigation he would need for his plantings. He planned his wheat field in his mind's eye and thought that he could even plant an orchard if he could only stay here long enough to see it grow to fruition. Fiona and Lars fervently hoped that they would not be ostracized and put out by yet another community because of their children.

Early that first spring, due to flooding in the lowlands to the north, Nia became overrun by fleeing rats. Fannie, even more so than Den, had a special connection to animals. She could understand the villagers' resentment toward the rodent infestation but she also sensed the rats' suffering as they were systematically sought out and killed. The villagers could not allow these ravenous rats to eat up their stored grains and vegetables so they hunted and destroyed as many of the dreadful creatures as they could find. Fannie felt the rats' pain as if it were her own.

While waiting for their parents to conclude their business and come out of the town's inn, one morning, Fannie and Den began to walk along the road that led out of town and toward the southern woods. Hand in hand, they made their way out of the community; many town folk witnessed an amazing event. The children seemed to emanate a faint light which attracted the rats from their hiding places. The vermin followed the children as they made their way into the woods. The children led the infestation away from the town and to the safety of the forest. The rats were gone, never to return. Although the folk who witnessed the supernatural event in Nia were pleased with the results, they feared and grew very suspicious of what the children could be capable of. The news spread quickly and before midday, the entire community was buzzing with rumours about the enchanted children. When she heard the gossip, Fiona shuddered to think that this would mean moving again.

Fiona had just confirmed that she was pregnant. She and Lars would be having a child of their own and she wanted this child to have a permanent home. Nia was the place she wanted to raise her son or her daughter. Fiona could not face the prospect of trying to establish herself in yet another community just so her adoptive children could force yet another move. She was also becoming increasingly afraid of her own children. As she and her husband made their way back to their farm that afternoon, Fiona pondered aloud to Lars about what might happen if the children should ever turn their powers against either of them or if they became jealous of the new baby. Lars was sympathetic to her fears but he reminded Fiona of their oath to look after the children. He reminded her how they loved the twins dearly and never wanted to see any harm come to either one of them. Lars always thought of the twins as his own and he believed that Fiona genuinely felt that way in her true heart. Lars assumed that Fiona's doubts and fears were manifesting themselves because she was with child.

Before Den and Fannie arrived home that night, the town elders visited Lars and his wife. The elders were a group of men who managed the business of the town of Nia. They settled squabbles and enforced the rules set by the community. After the spectacle with the rats that afternoon, this visit was not totally unexpected but it was not something Lars and Fiona looked forward to. The elders required no excuses or explanations. Martine, the head elder, made a proposal to the children's parents. The town elders had met in a hurried fashion after the twins had made their way into the forest and they had come to a unanimous decision. They insisted that the children could not remain as a part of the community. They had heard rumours and gossip from travelling performers about strange events that had occurred in other towns and villages. These stories always surrounded two children with strange eyes who had powers to control fire, calm storms and now they could apparently influence animals. The children were no longer welcomed because no one could predict what they may be capable of if they were somehow angered. This was magic and magic was not welcomed, especially in Nia. Lars and Fiona would be welcomed to come back and live in the village if they led their children off to the forest where they could easily be rid of them. Lars was a good farmer and his vegetables were often the juiciest and tastiest. Fiona was a midwife who had successfully attended several births during the time that they had lived in this particular town. The choice was theirs to make; be rid of the twins or move on, again.

Fiona begged Lars to listen to the elders. She became hysterical; she had been right about the twins. Even the elders agreed that they were dangerous. She didn't want to move again. She was pregnant. He was supposed to be a good husband and look after his wife. The haranguing went on and on for what seemed like eons to poor Lars. The sun was setting and the children would soon be home for the evening meal. Lars needed to find a solution to this dilemma that could satisfy the elders and Fiona without causing harm to his beautiful Den and Fannie.

Lars would not even consider leading his children off to die in the deep woods. There had to be another solution that would satisfy the elders and keep Fiona from losing all reason. Before the twins made their way home, the couple finally compromised. They agreed to travel to a far off town with the excuse of visiting a fair and when they found the opportunity, they would leave the children where they might at least have a chance to survive on their own. Lars was racked with guilt but he soothed his misery with the knowledge that Den and Fannie would not be abandoned in the wild. Once the arrangement was cleared with the elders and set in motion, things happened very quickly. The elders insisted that certain precautions be taken so that the twins could not find their own way back to Crerar. They made it clear that if the children returned there would be no second chance for

Fiona or Lars to stay in the community. The children would be drugged for the journey and left in a place so far form Crerar that returning would be impossible. Lars decided to journey to the city of Manek. The trip would take many days, even riding in a wagon which he would borrow from one of his sympathetic neighbours. Manek was a city of such great proportion that no one in Crerar could even imagine its extent. It was located on the Northern continent in the prosperous country of Adnak. This destination satisfied the elders and so the family prepared for their long voyage.

CHAPTER 2

LESS THAN A week went by before the family set out to visit a fair in far off Manek. Lars explains to his excited children that he had borrowed a wagon and two horses so that they could ride since the distance was so great. Lars spoke to the children about all of the exciting experiences that awaited them. They would see performers and hear storytellers. There would be an opportunity to buy seeds and plants that could be grown once they returned home. The children were very excited and grateful to be included in this special trip. Fiona prepared a special treat for the children that she generously laced with a medicinal substance often used to calm birthing mothers. It would make the children sleep through most of the voyage. Fiona did not want the children to be able to find their way home. If they had no idea of the direction that they had travelled, they would never find their way back. Lars agreed that this was a good idea but his reasons were quite different. He was a kind man and he continued to deal with the guilt from having agreed to such a cruel plan. Looking into the eyes of his adopted twins only made his remorse worse.

The family travelled for a fortnight and Den and Fannie only woke briefly to tend to their private matters and to eat light meals which continued to be laced with the sleeping potion. They cuddled together on a straw pallet in the rear of the wagon as they were driven further and further from the home they would probably never see again. The trip was both long and arduous, especially for Fiona who was quite obviously with child. She was uncomfortable and sore which only made her a very poor travelling companion. Lars became uncharacteristically quiet and his mood was less than pleasant.

The twins were confused and light-headed when they were finally allowed to wake from their drugged sleep. The city they saw through the slats in the back of the wagon was like a fairy tale. Even from a great distance, the city was like nothing they had ever seen or even imagined. The horizon was dominated by what appeared to be a great castle and the sheer size of the metropolis was mind boggling. The closer they came to the city the more fascinating things looked. The wagon crossed several bridges and then passed through a stone gate that was so great; the twins wondered how the huge stones could have been moved into place. Inside the gate, there were large houses and wide roads where two carts could easily pass one another with plenty of room left on either side for people who pushed barrows and walked. Neither Den nor Fannie had ever dreamed of such an amazing place. Even Lars and Fiona were taken aback by the grandeur and opulence of Manek. Den and Fannie crept up to the front of the wagon to sit with their parents so that they could gain a better view of all the things that fascinated. The houses had doors that were painted with bright colours. The windows were covered with a transparent substance which allowed those inside to look out without being exposed to the elements. These were truly splendid possessions. The children thought that such a place could only hold more marvels for them to discover.

    The cart rumbled through the city of Manek until they reached a less prosperous area. Lars drove the horses into a stable that was attached to a slanted wooden building where the family could barter for shelter while they conducted their business. A small stable boy rushed out to take charge of the wagon while the adults stretched their sore muscles after their long voyage. Den helped his father to take their few belongings into the building where they were led to a small room with one sleeping pallet and a small table with two stools. Den looked forward to staying in this inn where he and Fannie could snuggle in the pallet with their parents. Meanwhile, Fannie and her mother traded some preserved fruits that they had brought with them, for a warm dinner that would feed all four of them. Sitting beside a large fireplace in a darkened dining hall, they sat together and ate warm bread trenchers filled with rich brown gravy and small morsels of mutton. The food made them feel renewed and there were still a few hours of daylight left so the family made their way out of the inn and wandered toward the business area in this section of the city.

    The children took in the wonders of a real city. Just the sheer numbers of people awed them as they shuffled and rushed to keep up with their parents. At dusk, Lars and Fiona were thirsty and found a pub in a less than respectable area of Manek. Lars instructed the children to wait outside the pub just the way they waited for them back in Nia. They were to speak to no one until their parents came back out. Den and Fannie were thirsty as well, but they obeyed their parents and sat on the stoop to wait. Fannie noticed a small rain barrel at the side of the large building which housed the pub. A long drain pipe directed water from the roof to be collected in the barrel. It was meant to collect water for horses and possibly to clean the street but Den agreed that they could drink from the barrel to satisfy their rising thirsts. After satisfying their thirsts, they sat holding hands, waiting for their parents. Dusk turned into evening and evening into night. Fannie leaned into the crook of Den's arm and they both dozed on the hard stoop. They were hungry again and hoped that their parents would soon emerge with something to fill their empty bellies. As dawn broke and began to illuminate the jagged horizon of roofs and steeples, Den decided it was time to go into the pub and find his parents. They must have dozed off inside just as he and his sister had done on the outside.

Without speaking aloud, they decided to go into the pub together. The large wooden door had no window, only a smoothly worn handle that looked very large in Den's slender hand. He pulled the handle and then tried pushing against the door but it was most assuredly locked. Fannie wondered how the door could be locked when their parents were still inside. Den nodded gravely and gave Fannie a look of deep concern. Fannie's mind was full of trepidation and worry which immediately caused Den to feel the same way.

Together, they made their way around the side of the building where they noticed a small window covered with a cracked board. Den dragged a small crate to the window and hauled himself up. He was just tall enough to peek through the crack into the darkened pub. Standing in the gutter beside the crate, with her eyes gently shut, Fannie could see everything that Den saw. The pub was dirty and many of the tables were still littered with last evening's flotsam. The floor was strewn with straw that needed changing. There were overturned tankards and numerous jugs left scattered on the length of bar. The most important thing was that the bar was completely empty. Fiona and Lars were not dozing anywhere inside the pub nor was there another human being that they could speak to. Their parents were missing. The children began to panic and they both envisioned several horrible things that may have happened to their loving parents. They may have been injured, kidnapped, attacked . . . . killed.

Fannie began stepping over old bricks and piles of old boards as she began making her way toward the rear of the building. Den hopped off the crate and followed closely behind her. They both knew that their parents did not exit the public house through the front door so they agreed that they may find some clue to their disappearance in the back alley. The area behind the pub was dingy and unkempt. Garbage was piled high on one side of a small doorway and the other side was littered with large empty barrels and small kegs. The alley curved to the right so Den and Fannie could not see where it led or even if there was another exit. Fear and apprehension kept them from running along the eerie alley screaming for their parents.

Fannie tried the rear door and found that it was unlocked and easy to open. They both peered inside and slowly made their way into the gloom which shrouded the pub. No one in sight, they prowled around each table looking for something. Nothing. No indication that their parents had ever been here.

When Fiona and Lars entered the pub the previous evening they wasted no time sitting to quench their very real thirsts. They inquired at the bar about a rear exit and asked for directions so that they would not need to use the main street. The barman was not surprised that these people needed to escape from someone so he led them to the rear exit and pointed them toward the curve in the alley. Within minutes after entering the bar and even before Fannie and Den drank rainwater from the barrel, the couple were hurrying back toward the inn. They had marched the children in circles for most of the afternoon so they were not actually very far from the inn where their wagon waited for them. Lars took their few belongings from the room while Fiona traded more of their canned goods for some bread and cheese. They retrieved the horses and wagon and were on their way out of Manek before it was fully dark.

Through this ordeal, Lars became inundated with guilt and penitence but Fiona was less remorseful because she was more filled with fear and an overwhelming feeling of relief. Lars could not look his wife in the eye and although he knew he was just as responsible for his actions, he knew that he would never forgive Fiona for putting him in this situation. A man should never have to choose between his spouse and his children. His feelings for Fiona would never be the same and he foresaw that their lives would become hollow and sad without their beautiful twins.

All through the night Lars manoeuvred the wagon out of Manek and along the road that would lead him and Fiona back to their small village that was still many days journey. Fiona curled up in the back of the wagon next to the bags of potatoes that they brought along for roasting in the fire each evening when they stopped to sleep. As she slept soundly, Lars had time to think and he began to regret his decision more and more. His eyes filled with tears when he imagined Fannie and Den alone and afraid in that large city that was filled with unknown dangers. The following day, as the sun broke on the horizon, Lars turned the wagon and headed back toward Manek to find his children. He would have to deal with Fiona and the villagers later. He had driven most of the evening and the entire night so he was a long way from his children when they were standing back outside the pub in the gloomy back alley.

It was late morning when Fannie and Den gathered their courage and fought the rising panic that they shared. They came back out onto the street and tried to remember their way back to the inn. Their parents must be there. It was the only place they could think of to look for them. Neither of them realized the risk that two beautiful children must be taking by just walking alone on the streets of a big city. They were ignorant of the wickedness and evil that existed in the world to which they were newly arrived. First they walked but as they realized that they were completely turned around, and had passed this way already, they began to run. Running always attracts attention and Den was roughly grabbed by a huge burly man pushing a laden vegetable cart. The man supposed that Den was stealing. Fannie was frantic and felt just as though the monstrous hand that held Den was clamped around her own arm. She couldn't move but soon the giant released Den after he was satisfied that his pockets were empty and that he had stolen nothing. He growled at the children and said that running through the city would only lead to more trouble. Den and Fannie forced themselves to walk arm in arm trying to look as inconspicuous as possible. They spoke to each other in their secret way and kept their eyes averted to try to be invisible. They walked in this fashion for what seemed like days but it was actually not yet noon when they finally caught sight of the inn with the slanting stable.

They entered the inn and it was very busy, filled with people who were either coming or going or trying to procure their midday meal. Den and Fannie never let go of each other's hand while they quietly slipped up the steep stairway that led to the room they had been assigned the previous day. Empty. The sleeping pallet did not look like anyone had rested there at all. The children sank to the floor and held each other while hot tears ran down their cheeks and dripped from their chins. Alone. They had each other but otherwise they were alone.

They knew that they couldn't stay here so they sombrely stood and faced the door. They made their way down the stairs and through the crowded dining area. The stable was their next stop. No horses and no wagon. The children were devastated as they reasoned that their parents had left them not by accident but on purpose. The question of what to do next was ricocheting from Fannie's mind to Den's. They simultaneously accepted that they could not stay here. The city frightened them, especially after their encounter with the threatening vegetable vendor. As one, they decided to try to make their way out of the city and leave their precarious futures to chance where they could feel more at ease in familiar surroundings.

While the children were leaving the stable, Lars was facing a hysterical and defiant Fiona. She had woken shortly after Lars had turned the wagon back towards Manek. It was several minutes, while she stretched and came fully awake, before she realized that the wagon was heading north. They should be headed south. That was where their futures awaited them. Without the twins, they could live a happy and quiet life with neighbours who accepted and valued them. Lars was trying to ruin everything that Fiona schemed to accomplish. She tried to reason with Lars and finally ended up raging at him. Finally, she jumped off the wagon, expecting Lars to stop and listen to her but she was surprised when the wagon kept rolling along the rutted road. To her disbelief, Lars simply slowed the wagon but did not direct the horses to stop. In her pregnant state, Fiona hiked up her skirts and gave chase. The speed of the wagon allowed her to catch up and eventually hike herself up onto the front seat beside her sombre and strangely quiet husband. Lars refused to respond to anything Fiona said and as the hours passed, the recently estranged couple made their way slowly northward toward the place where they had abandoned their adopted twins. Lars pondered how he could ever have considered and then have agreed to leave those defenceless children to their own devices without even a copper to buy bread or hard cheese. Silently, he fervently prayed that they would find Den and Fannie safe so that he could tell them how sorry he was for his heinous behaviour.

CHAPTER 3

DEN WAS THINKING hard about their first wagon ride into this maze of a city. Fannie filled in many recounted details as they tried to remember the way that would take them back to the road, banked with woods on either side. They walked and passed many of the landmarks that they held in their memories. The double red doors trimmed in a blue colour so dark it appeared almost black. They passed the house with the covered windows followed by the stone gate with a passage so wide that three carts could pass through at the same time. They crossed a stone bridge that spanned a fast moving stream.

Most of the day had passed and the children were sore, hungry, thirsty and tired. Once they had walked across the bridge, they decided to shimmy down the bank to reach the fresh water. It was cool and refreshing and it was all they had with which to fill their empty stomachs. Den cradled Fannie and they both lay down on the bank to rest. Within moments they were both asleep just under the bridge where they were out of sight. As the twins slept, Lars urged the horses over that very bridge on his way back to the city to try to find his children. This was the closest Fiona and Lars would ever come to reuniting with their children.

It was dark when the children stirred awake. In the city it had been chilly while they spent the night waiting for their parents in front of the pub but outside of the city it was really very cold. They shivered and used the water in the stream to clean their faces and drink their fill. They were still too devastated to make any rational decisions about their circumstances but they did know that they were hungry. They climbed the bank and resumed their course toward the south . . . home?

Many people used this road and they passed several others walking and many more people pushing or riding in small carts or wagons. Villagers were bringing their fruits and vegetables to the city. Vendors travelled with goods of every kind to be sold to consumers who made the city their home. Those who travelled the road away from the city were pulling empty carts; their goods had already been sold. Eventually a dusty looking farmer trundled toward the children with a nearly empty wagon. He was a good man, lonely since his wife had died. His heart was touched when he spied the beautiful children with their raven curls that reminded him of his dear Patrice. He slowed his wagon as he neared the twins and offered them a ride and their fill of the apples that he was unable to sell at the market. They smiled at him and his heart melted. Jok introduced himself and told the children that he had a farm less than a day's ride to the west. Fannie's feet were very sore and Den could feel her pain. They accepted the ride and the apples but they were reluctant to tell Jok too much about themselves. They could sense that he was a good man so they told him their names and made pleasant conversation during their ride to Jok's farm. He talked at length about his wife, Patrice. She was beautiful and good, a loving wife who was thrilled to give Jok his first child. She had black hair with wild curls that could not be controlled. He had a tear in his eye when he spoke about her. She promised him a son who would have her curls and his kind heart. Alas, it was not to be. His son would not be born and mother and child went to their next life together on the night that Jok should have become a proud father. The twins were shaken and deeply moved by Jok's story. They were both taken with his soft smile, his heartfelt story and his generosity toward two strange children lost on a road.

They arrived at Jok's farm and were pleasantly surprised to find a meticulously tended barn where they helped Jok to unhitch, water and feed his horses. Jok stored the wagon and invited the children to come to the house. He apologized that there was no stew bubbling over the fire because he lived alone and it would be hours before he could offer a warm dinner. His neighbour had come in daily to feed the animals so they were taken care of for the day. Inside, he could offer some flat bread and hard cheese and of course, apples. As they followed him toward the house they passed Jok's vegetable garden that rivalled any garden their father had ever planted. They could not even name some of the exotic looking vegetables that flourished here. After passing by the garden, the children were amazed to see row upon row of miniature apple trees. The trees were so short that even Fannie could pick the fruit from the highest branch without a stool or ladder. These trees were laden with large juicy apples. Some were red and plump and some were just as large but the colour of fresh grass. Jok smiled when he noticed that they were admiring his orchard. He was very proud of his apples; they were the best fruit in the area. Jok pointed in the other direction, just behind the house where the twins saw Jok's berry patch. Strawberries, raspberries, gooseberries, blueberries, pokeberries and fizzle root all flourished side by side. Beyond the berry patch, Jok had a small orchard of various fruit and nut trees. Den recognised some of them because he loved peaches and pecans but some of the others were a mystery to him. On their way around the house, Jok took a moment to collect several peaches and a handful of nuts that neither Fannie nor Den recognized. Without apprehension, the decision was made, the children would stay for dinner with Jok and they would see where fate guided them afterwards.

Good fortune was with the children when they found Jok. He was more than he explained but he was a good man and his feelings for the children were pure and decent.

Fannie and Den spent a week with Jok. They followed him as he did the chores required to keep his farm in order. They helped with anything they could and the three became fast friends. Jok still didn't know any of the children's secrets because they were afraid to confide in him lest he turn them out if he learned that even their own parents didn't want them. They had come to accept that they had been abandoned by Lars and Fiona and this was still very difficult for them to deal with. They had loved their parents unconditionally and could not believe that they would just leave them. During their silent conversations Den determined that it was the special powers everyone attributed to Fannie and himself that had been the reason they were shunned and abandoned. It was also quite obvious that they could never try to find their parents. They did not want their children back. They vowed to never show or use the powers that they themselves didn't even understand. Their silent communication was the only power they would allow themselves. Although they were determined, this was not a promise that they would be able to keep for very long.

How long could they stay with Jok? His farmhouse had plenty of room and was actually much nicer than any house they had ever seen. They stayed in a bedroom with two small beds that Jok fashioned for them during their first week's stay. Their mattresses were stuffed with fresh smelling straw and their blankets were soft and warm. Jok asked little in return for all of his hospitality but Den insisted that they begin to do assigned jobs around the farm. Jok was anxious for the children to stay because they had already occupied a large part of his big heart. Fannie appointed herself as the chief cook and house keeper while Den took charge of the animals. Den groomed and milked, fed and tended the cows, goats, chickens and pigs. He collected the eggs and delivered them to Fannie who cooked and baked for the makeshift family. Apple Cobbler soon became one of Fannie's specialities. Jok was very pleased to see the children relax and enjoy farm life. The twins chose never to leave the farm when Jok made trips to barter with his apples and other produce. They stayed and tended the animals and always had a pot of bubbling stew ready for Jok when his cart came rumbling back down the long track. Life went on this way for more than a year. Den and Fannie missed their parents less and less as the time passed and they eventually stopped blaming them for the abandonment.

CHAPTER 4

DEN AND FANNIE were ten years old and Fannie was blooming into a lovely young woman. Her fine features and milky complexion set off by those long black curls made her look fragile. Den was the male counterpart of his sister. He was taller but also slight of build and he possessed an ethereal quality. In the evenings, when Jok and the children sat by the fire, Jok sometimes stared at Fannie and remembered his fair Patrice. His mind was so wide open and honest that Den found that he could often get an impression of what Jok was feeling. It was on one of these evenings that Fannie received a full blown message from Jok and it shocked her. She was accustomed to hearing her brother's thoughts in her head but she had never experienced anyone else's mind. Fannie's mind was always wide open to Den so he also found his way into Jok's thoughts. Jok projected his longing for Patrice and his love for her had not diminished since her untimely death. They also experienced his loneliness, the kind that could only be cured by the love of a woman. Jok wanted happiness for the children but he also wanted children of his own. He mourned his son and he longed for another. With access to Jok's inner most thoughts, the children probed him and found that he was everything that he presented. He was a virtuous man and they loved him. They sent him soothing thoughts to comfort him for his loss and happy thoughts to lessen his suffering. This all happened in a split second but the children made a decision at that same moment. They would confide in Jok. He had become as much a father to them as anyone had ever been.

They planned to tell him their secret when he returned from the trip he had scheduled for the following morning. He would be away for a few days, making deliveries and purchasing those things that they needed on the farm. He had promised to bring Fannie a new green frock that would bring out her lovely complexion. Den needed a few new tools which were also on Jok's list.

The few days passed without incident and Den and Fannie were excited to share their mystery with Jok upon his return. He did not return on the evening when they expected him. Three more days passed and the twins were beyond worry. From the kitchen, Fannie finally heard the cart coming toward the barn and her relief was palpable; Den heard her thoughts and rushed in from the orchard to greet Jok.

Jok was not alone. He hopped down from the wagon in his jaunty manner and offered a hand to help a young woman step lightly down to the dry ground. She was striking, just slightly taller than Fannie but she had long blond hair and aquiline features. Her smile was genuine when she glanced toward Fannie and Den. Jok proudly introduced El to the children and informed them that she was to become his wife. Had Jok really found a woman to take Patrice's place in his heart? Fannie could feel his happiness and she just hoped that El would fulfill all of Jok's desires. This explained the additional days that kept Jok away. There was no need to question him or let him know about their worry. Their plans to confide in Jok were put on hold.

The four made their way toward the house and Fannie and Den did all that they could to make El welcomed. She had yet to say a word and the children were puzzled at her lack of manners. Jok spoke to the children as they made their way through the yard and explained that El was deaf and mute. Her family was looking for a good match for her but her disability made her a poor prospect. El's father had been one of Jok's customers for several years. Jok had watched as El matured form a gangly adolescent into a lovely young woman. During this visit with Jok, El's father confided his doubts about gaining a match for El. Jok knew that he could come to love El and he also knew that she would be a loving companion for the children. He fervently hoped that she would also have his children. His only concern centred on not really knowing if El really wanted to be his wife or if her father had forced her into this arrangement. The children sympathized with Jok and they felt his apprehension that he kept securely in his mind. With their access to his thoughts, the twins knew Jok as well as he knew himself.

The wedding took place on the edge of the orchard the following spring. It was a festive occasion and Fannie outdid herself with the celebration feast. By this time, Fannie and El had become fast friends and they worked well together in the kitchen. Fannie was eleven and El was seventeen. They were more like sisters and they treated each other as equals. Fan and El helped each other to dress in their wedding garb. Fannie wore the green frock that Jok had brought her last fall and El wore a white wedding frock which Fannie trimmed with tiny sprigs of Tal leaves. These leaves were attached to the frock for good luck.

El was nervous and she communicated this through the elaborate set of signals that the girls had devised to be able to converse. El's heightened emotional state and her close and trusting relationship with Fannie made the next event possible. Suddenly, and without warning, Fannie could hear El speaking inside of her head. She had forged a connection but this was different from the way Fannie heard Jok. In this case, El could hear Fannie too. They were both flabbergasted and it took some moments before they could compose themselves. By the time they were calmed down, Den came racing into the sleeping room where Fannie was dressing El for the wedding. He could hear Fannie, so he could also hear El. Den could not speak to El directly but she spoke to him through Fannie. El did not understand what was happening but she was delighted and fascinated to finally be able to speak and hear, even if it all happened inside her head. Den convinced El that this had to stay between the three of them because friends and neighbours would not understand this strange magic and they would be feared, probably shunned and possibly sent away. They told El how they had been able to communicate this way since birth and that they could read and hear Jok's thoughts as well. The problem was that they had decided to confide in Jok but they never gotten the opportunity since El arrived. After the wedding, they would all sit down and explain things to Jok. They knew that he loved them all and would understand and keep their secret. With this decision made, Den made his way outside to gather the guests for the ceremony.

Several of Jok's neighbours attended the nuptials as did El's father and brother, Frederer. El's mother was too weak to make the journey and she cared little for her daughter. Frederer was very close to his baby sister and cared deeply for her happiness. He was satisfied that Jok was a good man and was pleased that he lived within a day's ride so that he could visit often. Frederer knew that Jok would always be prosperous. With his gift for growing all manner of fruits and vegetables, his sister would never go without those things that she needed.

The wedding was a great success. Everybody danced and frolicked late into the night. Many of Jok's neighbours staggered to their carts and were probably still intoxicated when they reached their homes. Jok insisted that the clean up could wait for the morning and he swept his new bride off of her feet and carried her into the bedroom that they would share for the rest of their happy lives. El sent Fannie the last message for the night. It was a feeling of utter contentment and happiness. Den and Fannie were very happy for El and Jok.

The following morning El came into the kitchen to see the children and Jok in a serious conversation. She communicated with Fannie and realized that Jok had been told about their special powers. He seemed to need a moment to take it all in but slowly a wide smile appeared on his face. His first thought centred on whether he would be able to speak to El. If Fannie and Den could hear his thoughts, was it possible for all four of them to somehow link so that he could really speak to El? Den said that they could try but he admitted that they really didn't know how to control or initiate their powers. They tried all morning to link El with Jok but it was not to be. Jok's disappointment was deep but he was still pleased that El had someone to talk to, even if it wasn't him. Fannie explained to Jok that she might able to project El's feelings to him the same way that she had sent him love and happiness the day he had been mourning his Patrice.

Fannie linked with El and found the feelings that she felt for Jok. She then projected those feelings to Jok, whose eyes filled with tears. He hugged El and thanked the children for making it possible for him to know her feelings since she would never be able to actually tell him. He truly loved El with his whole heart and it meant everything to him to know that she felt the same way.

Life on the farm was bliss. Before long, El's belly showed the signs of what everybody already knew; Jok would have a son or a daughter. They would need a midwife and the need brought back memories for the children. Their adoptive mother had been a skilled midwife but Fannie had still been too young to have learned any of her craft. As her time grew close, Jok travelled to the city to sell and trade his crop. He made arrangements for a midwife to come and stay at the farm to deliver the child that was expected any day.

As it happened, Jok and the midwife were late arriving. By the time Jok's cart was heard in the laneway, El was close to death from loss of blood and the child was blue for lack of breath. The midwife took over as soon as she entered the kitchen but she said it was too late. The infant and the mother were not long for this world. Jok's agony slammed into the twins' minds like an avalanche. Fannie and Den could not let this happen to El, and especially not to Jok! Not again.

El had been kneading the dough that Fannie prepared to bake fresh buns for the evening meal. Her first labour pain coincided with her water breaking. From that moment her pains came fast and furious. She was brave but as the hours passed and as Fannie nursed and encouraged her, she knew that something was terribly wrong. Den had delivered many litters of piglets and even a calf. He knew that the child was shifted and was in the wrong position for birthing. What he did not know was that the birthing cord was wrapped tightly about the child's neck. He and Fannie did everything that they could think of to ease the birth but they had little experience. Fannie tried to massage El's belly and by some miracle the baby adjusted its position so that its head began to emerge. By now, El was exhausted and had little strength left to push the child from her fatigued womb. Her child emerged a moment before Jok and Edna, the midwife, arrived on the scene. Edna took control of the situation but her prognosis left little hope for either mother or child.

Jok howled his anguish and this caused the children to react without thinking of the consequences. They had made a solemn promise to avoid using their powers, especially where strangers could spread tales and gossip. They did not know this midwife but they could not let El slip away nor could they allow the child to go without a lifesaving breath. Fannie and Den joined hands and laid their other hands on the baby. A violet aura surrounded the twins and enveloped the child. Within moments the child was howling a protest to being born. It was the loveliest sound they could have heard. Edna rushed to swaddle the infant lest he catch a chill and she announced that he was a boy. El tried to sit up so that she could glimpse her son but she was so completely weakened by her ordeal that she was barely clinging to life. Her lifeblood was pouring out of her as Jok cradled her in his arms. The twins moved to El's side and as she struggled to project her thoughts, Den and Fannie understood that El's last wish was for the welfare of her new son; his name should be Mica. They sent El soothing emotion and they made silent vows to love Mica but they had no intention of letting El die. They both sent her strength as then they laid their hands on her belly causing their fingers to touch. The same violet aura enveloped them and El took her first full lungful of air. The colour returned to her face and she smiled. The midwife took in all the happenings and seemed unafraid and only somewhat surprised. Edna handed the child to El and demanded that she would still require her payment. Jok was beside himself. His relief was impossible to measure and he would have paid her double if she had requested it. He gave her the necessary coins and asked Den to provide her with a horse and saddle which could be counted as part of her payment. He wanted her sent on her way before she could even think to ask questions about the children. As it happened, she had seen enough and needed to ask no questions. News of these children would travel with her and she would be sure that the right people knew where to find them. The rewards for such information were generous and she was tiring of this midwifery. With a minimum of conversation, Den saw Edna on her way and rushed back to the house to see if he could be of further service.

There was no need to hurry. The kitchen was a mess but Fannie, Jok and El were all smiling as Mica announced his existence with squeals that could be heard as far as the barn. He was alive and healthy and his mother would live to nurse him and love him. The fertile country of Adnak had its newest citizen and his father hoped that one day he too would become a prosperous farmer.

Thoughts of Edna faded in the children's memories and they enjoyed a happy life on the farm with Jok and El and especially Mica. He was a joy to everybody. He was at the crawling stage when El announced that Mica would soon have a brother or a sister. El's daughter was born without complications. Nina looked just like Mica. They were both spitting images of their father. Their hair was fair and their features were dominated by their beautiful blue eyes, so pale that they seemed transparent.

Turning thirteen was a special occasion. The twins would no longer be considered children; they would be adults in the eyes of the law. Jok teased Fannie that he would soon have to negotiate for a marriage match for her. Jok encouraged Den to come on the trips with him so that he could begin to meet the girls that would be available for him in the near future. Den didn't know how to inform Jok that he was a long way from being interested in settling down to farm and raise a family. Den always had a nagging suspicion that his life would take him in a direction he had not yet seen. He was very sure that Fannie would be a part of that phantom life that could not yet be identified. Den treasured each day he spent on Jok's farm because he inwardly knew that those days were numbered. Fannie shared all of Den's thoughts so she was also convinced that another destiny awaited them.

CHAPTER 5

WINTER ON THE northern continent could be harsh but this year it was exceptionally brutal. The growing season did not come till late in the spring and the planting was late. It was the coldest winter that Fannie and Den had ever experienced. Having lived their first nine years on the southern continent, they were unaccustomed to the harsh climate. Stories had made their way up from the south that even they were having weather changes. Many of the tropical fruit trees had perished from the cold and the frost that had blanketed them for days on end. Jok's orchard was suffering its own problems. The apple harvest would be late and if winter came early again, there might be no harvest at all. The family prepared for a long winter by drying, storing and canning as many ripe fruits and vegetables as possible. Fannie visited all of the hives and collected enough honey to sweeten hundreds of apple pies and cobblers. Jok also liked his tea sweet so Fannie was sure to collect more than she expected to use. Potatoes and turnips were stored in barrels and carried deep into the cellar where they would remain fresh. Den stored barrels of nuts in the cold cellar where they would be kept dry and away from the freezing temperatures. Jok's family would be fine but many of their neighbours would have a difficult time keeping enough food on the table if things did not improve. The farmers always looked to their own needs first and any lack of marketable foods would affect cities like Manek first. No one was predicting a shortage as of yet but time would tell.

The spring thaw brought Jok another son that El named Frederer, after her brother. They also received a very strange visitor. She just ambled down the laneway one afternoon and asked if the farm could spare some cool water and a light repast for a weary traveller. Jok was never one to turn anyone away so he invited her in to join them for their midday meal. She took an uncommon interest in Den and Fannie from the moment that she met them. The twins were now fourteen and ever since their encounter with Edna, the midwife, they had been suspicious of strangers who came to the farm. There were many occasional visitors but this woman set off alarms in both Den and Fannie. Her name was Carlotta and she seemed to be trying to read their thoughts. The twins protected their minds from any kind of probe but they both felt like somebody was flitting around the edges of their thoughts. El felt it too, even though she could not project to anyone but Fannie. Carlotta spent the night in the barn loft and was on her way the following day but she left everyone with a feeling of apprehension and anxiety. Carlotta followed the road toward the capital, Manek, where she planned to meet with some others who could do magic. They were all part of a secret society that searched out those of their kind. If these people had come across the twins when they were only nine years old and lost in the big city, they would have been well schooled in the magic arts by their fourteenth birthday. Instead, The Society had paid a considerable weight of coin to a midwife who came to report the twins' existence. With many reported cases in need of investigation, Carlotta had taken a while to visit Jok's farm to determine whether or not the children were worth their while. Now that she had met them, seen their eyes and determined that they were twins, they had become her prime interest. Every day that they spent in their mundane lives on the farm was a waste of valuable time in which they could be schooled to become so much more.

CHAPTER 6

THE CAPITAL CITY of Manek was much larger than the twins knew. They had only experienced a small part of the south end of the sprawling metropolis. Over the years, the city had continued to grow at such a steady rate that there were ten rings of city gates found within the city itself. Each time the city burst beyond its current walls, new walls were built. This had happened ten times in the last 300 years. Den and Fannie had only passed into the most outer ring of the city, having never ventured into the older sections. The city occupied a piece of land that jutted out into the sea so that three sides of the metropolis faced the water. The city was divided into four sections, Northman, Southman, Eastman and The Western Coast. Although Northman and Southman both had short coastlines, the main trading ports were all located in the Western Coast. The shipyards, where all the building took place, were all on the Northman coast. The palace that belonged to the reigning royal family of Adnil, the Northern continent, was located in the Southman area of Manek. It was built against the coastline and could be seen from a great distance when approaching Manek by sea. It was constructed entirely of black marble, trimmed with white and pink marble. The royal family had always lived on the island of Solosk until an aging King decreed that a palace should be constructed at the seaport of Manek to make it easier for the court to entertain those dignitaries that visited Adnak. The building took several generations and provided work for a myriad of architectural planners and educated thinkers who could envision the needs of those who would occupy the palace. The plans even included water that ran both freely and through pipes built into the castle walls to make life more pleasant. Some rooms even housed baths large enough for swimming. Peasants travelled from far and wide to work as stone cutters and sculptors. Many people who live in Manek were only there because their great great grandfathers had come to pour their sweat into the toil that built the castle and the great city.

Manek itself was almost as large as a small country and was populated with half as many people as the entire southern continent. The country of

Adnak, with its mountains in the east and the sea to the west was blessed with an ideal climate to grow almost any type of grain, fruit and vegetable. The industrious farmers of Adnak produced more than enough food to supply the great demands made by its capital city. Fresh water flowed through a myriad or rivers that emerged from the mountains and irrigated the fertile soil on their way to the sea. Their waters were harnessed along the way to turn the giant wheels of the grist mills which ground wheat and corn. Barges moved slowly down the wide rivers to deliver their cargo to side ports and eventually to the main port at Manek. Roads were built so that the goods required by the city could be easily transported from the farms that dotted the countryside for leagues around the great city.

The richest aristocrat and the lowliest beggar both called Manek home although their paths seldom crossed. Many thousands of people lived out their entire lives within a single section of the city. All manner of goods and services were required so people were employed and coin changed hands so that most people could afford their needs. There was no need to ever leave the city, everything they needed was available somewhere close by.

Carlotta was hot and exhausted by the time she neared the outskirts of Manek. Once she entered the outer gates, she could hire a runner with a seat cart to pull her to her destination. If only she could abide horses or even donkeys, she wouldn't have to walk everywhere she went. Even being in close proximity to the wretched beasts sent her into fits of sneezing and caused her skin to develop welts and lesions. She had tried a number of potions to curb the affliction but thus far horses were not her friends. The night she had spent in Jok's barn, in the loft located just above the horses' stalls, had not been pleasant. She recovered from the sneezing and then endured three days walking along the road that skirted the south side of the river which emptied into the sea just south of Manek. With the Southman gates finally in sight she breathed a sigh of relief. Within 3 hours she would be soaking in a tub of warm water scented with rosehips.

A tall muscled Cormian leaned on the cool stone wall just inside the gate with his shaded seat cart waiting for a customer. His dark skin was well oiled and his muscles stood out on his chiselled torso. Men from Cormer were the fastest runners and Carlotta was very relieved to see him standing there and very anxious to hire him. In no time at all Carlotta was comfortably seated and speeding through the city toward the castle. From this direction the western horizon was dominated by the silhouette of the castle which appeared almost black with the sun setting behind it. Carlotta loved being back in the city. She cherished every sight and smell. The bustle, the crowds, the noise and the flavour; these were the things she missed while roaming through the countryside. This is where she enjoyed all that life had to offer and this was the place where she had always been happiest.

No longer a young woman, Carlotta faired well for her 27 years. She had never married because she chose to follow her aunt into The Society. Her father's sister was a mysterious and stunning woman who had always fascinated Carlotta. When she visited her brother, little Carlotta followed her everywhere and always showed a keen interest in the things that her Aunt Eudora talked about. As she grew into adolescence, Carlotta had no interest in living a life like that of her parents. Even when she turned 14 she was reluctant to accept any matches that her father arranged for her and when she turned 16 he finally gave up. Eudora rescued Carlotta from a life of shame and drudgery by taking her away and placing her with The Society. Carlotta was 16 years of age when she was first introduced to The Society.

The Society started out as a small group of individuals who held a high respect for the magical arts. Magic itself had been around since the days before counting but those who could practice the arts, in this age, were few and far between. Common folk were naturally superstitious and usually feared and often ostracized anyone who even seemed connected to magic. Hags who sold or bartered their healing and love potions were tolerated and sometimes even respected by the communities that they serviced but these wily witches took care to distance themselves from any real kind of magic. The Society was formed to educate and protect those individuals who were truly gifted in the magical arts. Carlotta's Aunt Eudora was such a person. Her gifts were numerous and once she was schooled to control and focus her abilities she became a formidable practitioner of the Magical arts.

CHAPTER 7

THE CURRENT RULING member of the royal family of Adnil was a young Queen named Zelebeth. Her husband, Prince Archer, came from the split country of Locan, located far to the east and split between the southern and northern continents. He was tall and handsome, with long chestnut curls which framed his angular face. When he stood beside her, he dwarfed Zelebeth who was diminutive and fragile. Her complexion was very fair and her waist length hair was almost black and very curly. Her most redeeming feature was the deep violet colour of her eyes. Their marriage had been arranged only days after Zelebeth's birth but once they were allowed to meet, they were enamoured with each other and quickly discovered that they would enjoy a life filled with love. Most arranged marriages, especially within the aristocratic circles, were strictly political and did not concern themselves with the couple finding personal fulfillment or gratification. In this case, Zelebeth and Archer were very fortunate because they truly loved one another. The country flourished under the rule of the blissful young couple. Archer was 19 years old and Zelebeth was crowned ruling queen that very year at the age of 16.

Zelebeth's father, King Gaylord, was badly injured in a hunting accident near the border of Madyar and died soon afterwards. He had often travelled to Madyar, a country which occupied more than half of the peninsula northwest of Adnil. He had been hunting the elusive Giant White Bear found only in the far north. He died well before his time and Zelebeth found herself crowned Queen much sooner than she had expected. Zelebeth's mother, Queen D'Enfanel, had a difficult time giving birth to Zelebeth's sibling and after losing the boy child, she never recovered. The Queen lived for only a short time after she delivered the stillborn child and she was never again the woman she had been before her ordeal. The King raised his little princess from the time she was 3 years of age. She was taught to be compassionate, fair, tolerant and honest. The King hoped that wisdom would come to her naturally if she lived a virtuous life. King Gaylord took a keen personal interest in the magical arts and he was actually the main reason why The Society was allowed to flourish in Manek. Before being welcomed by the King, The Society did their work in secret to avoid persecution. His Queen had hated magic so it was only after her untimely death that The Society came to be housed in large buildings on the castle grounds. The chancellor of the Society had urged the King to allow them to prepare potions and fashion amulets to help cure the Queen when she was suffering from her malady but she would have nothing to do with anything magic. She did not want to die but her fear of magic may well be the reason she went to the next life well before her time.

After his Queen died, the King was a busy man so Princess Zelebeth spent much of her free time with the magicians who loved her and pampered her at every opportunity. The buildings where The Society was housed were opulent compared to the way most people lived. The King spared no expense to keep his magical friends comfortable and well fed. They swam in heated pools and slept on feather mattresses. Their walls were hung with all manner of tapestries carried to Manek from as far as the Desert Peninsula of Cordon. They had access to all manner of compounds necessary for their potions. The King allowed them to use gold, silver and gems from his treasury to fashion talismans and amulets. The King's only stipulation was that The Society would only ever work toward the greater good. If any individual was ever found to be working magic for reasons of greed or evil, they would be made to face the most heinous of consequences. This stipulation suited the Society because they were a virtuous group who plied only white magic. The dark arts were well documented but those secrets were kept very secure lest the information fall into the wrong hands. Only a select few had access to the libraries where the texts for the dark arts were kept. Those libraries were protected by charms and incantations which would make it impossible for anyone to enter without permission.

The Society actively sought out new recruits and invited them to live in fine style while they were schooled in the magical arts so that their skills could be studied and finely honed. Since King Gaylord had accepted The Society and his daughter continued to hold his opinion, numerous magicians had made themselves known. They had travelled from far and wide to join the Court of this indulgent King. Now Zelebeth was their host. This onslaught of new recruits, many of whom required much tutoring and instruction had caused The Society to become somewhat lax in their background investigations. The Society's chancellor, Morgan, felt a growing concern about some of his newer recruits. He inwardly noted that there were several cliques forming which included many new arrivals and excluded those who had been at the palace for a long time. Although this aroused some suspicion in the Chancellor, he vowed to keep an eye on the situation and address the matter only if it became necessary. He would live to regret that decision. Several of the new arrivals were taking advantage of the knowledge that the Society provided and worked hard to hone their personal skills while gathering information for those who had sent them to Manek. A lanky young man named Carl was such a spy. His hair was straight and usually greasy. Most often he could be found hunching in a doorway whispering to his small group of compatriots. Thus far, Carl's skills included dominion over fire and hypnotic suggestion. Where a fire existed, Carl, like his master, could control it. He was unable to start a fire from naught, accept in the normal fashion, but once he had but a spark, he could make the fire do what he commanded. Carl could also cause individuals to be convinced to do or say things that were not in their normal character. His use of hypnosis was well refined before he left his homeland of Afshen, and this was how he managed to gather a group of new Society recruits to do his bidding. Carl had ventured to Manek to seek out The Society and learn its secrets so that one day his masters could use this information for their own dark purposes. Magicians and sorcerers are a very patient breed and they take pleasure in casting their webs and planning their evil doings. Carl was only 15 years old but already his heart was dark and his intentions were rarely noble. Carl had his small sect listening for any tidbit of information that he could pass on to those who waited and planned in the north. He was skulking near the castle gate when he spotted a cart runner, fast approaching with a passenger resting behind a sun shade. Maybe this would be his lucky day.

Carlotta had arrived to report her find to The Society. She had found a set of twins who were untrained but very powerful. She had been able to skirt their minds and although she could not make contact with them while they protected their thoughts, she sensed that they were communicating with each other. Added to the witness account provided by Edna, Carlotta was sure that the twins would be invited to come to The Society. It was a shame that they were so old. Youngsters were always much easier to train because they put up much less resistance.

Carlotta was anxious to file her report so that she could soak her wary bones in a warm bath and then sleep on a real bed. She paid the Cormian his due coppers and began to make her way toward the main building. Carl fell in step with her and made sure to put on a happy smile when he welcomed her home. They made their way past the dormitories which housed all of the newer recruits and Carl convinced Carlotta to take a short pause to soak her swollen feet in one of the small fountains that were located in each courtyard. Once they sat down and cooled their feet, Carlotta was no longer in a hurry to do anything. Carl was keeping her subdued and relaxed till he could garner any important information she may be here to report. Carlotta had no reason to suspect Carl of any complicity so she spoke freely about her discovery. The twins were spectacular. They were completely unschooled but they were able to rebut her attempts to probe their thoughts. They showed all the physical signs of magic users, especially their green and violet eyes. After all, most of the most powerful wizards and sorcerers were twins. Carl took in all the information that Carlotta willingly shared. She told him the entire account made by Edna and she added in some tales she had heard from travelling performers coming back from Darmor, on the southern continent. In Crerar, they had heard stories about a set of twins who could control animals, cause fire to stop burning and even influence the weather. Carlotta vehemently hoped that these were the same twins. Once Carl had heard enough, he ceased his hypnosis and Carlotta was again agitated and eager to make her report to the Chancellor. She couldn't understand why she had wasted so much time resting at the fountain. She bid Carl farewell and marched herself directly to the main building. Carl made his way toward the rookery where he planned to ink a message and send it off as soon as possible. A strong bird should be able to reach the enclave at North Point in less than 4 days.

CHAPTER 8

ICE PORT WAS the only inhabited area colder than North Point but it could never be cold enough for Vigour. He loved the cold above all else. Freezing, frosty, icy, bitter, arctic and especially winter were all of his favourite things. His Achilles heel was heat. He was the most powerful practitioner of the dark arts by far. Even his name meant strength but he could still be defeated by something as simple as heat. This, of course was a closely guarded secret, known only to a very select few. Many who had known or guessed Vigour's secret fell victim to unfortunate accidents that resulted in their untimely demises. At present, Lily, V's wife and Moira, his closest confidant and sometimes concubine were the only living people to know this clandestine information.

V collected magic users in the same way as the Society did. He did not always live in the far north and hoped that Afshen would not be his final home.

When he was a young man he had faced all of the challenges any magician encountered. Magic had been frowned upon and even banned before the King had accepted The Society. Vigour, or V as he preferred to be called, did his best to live a normal life. He had hidden his powers with a great measure of success and even managed to marry a woman that he truly loved. He inherited a shoe making shop from his Uncle and began to run the business himself. He prospered and was well respected in the city of Messo. V expected his life to take a natural course. He wanted children and he accepted that he would have to work hard to provide for his family. His abilities with magic were sporadic at best but encompassed numerous skills. He possessed dominion over fire, earth and water; this was very rare in one individual.

Darina loved Vigour as fiercely as he loved her. They had tried to have children but it was not to be. Darina was an artisan who worked with silks and dyes to produce beautiful hangings and even clothing. Her work was sought after by the aristocracy as far away as Manek. After closing his shop, V would walk down to the wharf where Darina rented space to dry her fabric creations. This particular evening, the sky was dark and the winds blew strongly from the south. V knew from experience that this would be an extraordinary storm. He could feel all the hair on his arms and at the back of his neck stand on end; such was the electricity in the air. As he rounded the building his view of the waves crashing into the barricades blocking off the lagoon sent his pulse racing. Vigour needed to fetch Darina and get home before the storm hit with its full force. When the lightening struck the warehouse, Vigour was thrown over the balustrade and into the lagoon. The water was rough, even in the protected lagoon and it took all of this will and strength to forge his way to shore. The current had pushed him a good ways along the beach and from this distance he could see the warehouse burning out of control. He ran using every bit of energy he had. Like a madman he raced toward the flaming wharf. Using his magic never occurred to him, not till much later. He was much too late to save Darina from a fiery death; he did manage to almost die with her. His skin crisped when he reached the wharf and he would have died there and then if the wharf had not collapsed and thrown him back into the sea. He was pulled from the waves by onlookers who were drawn outdoors to watch the blazing inferno which was devouring the warehouse district. He was treated for his burns and the sea had saved him from death. No amount of healing or magic would ever rid the once handsome Vigour of the scars he now wore. Every time he saw his own reflection he would remember Darina and the fire that changed the course of his life. As soon as he was strong enough to travel, Vigour sold all his holdings and set of for a cooler climate. For no known reason he could no longer abide the warm breezes that blew in from the Inland Sea. He ventured north in search of a cool place to live out his wretched life. Vigour made his way to Kazmeel but was still not satisfied with the summers which allowed people to dress in light jackets to stay warm. He crossed the entire Prain Territory and crossed the divide. As he journeyed, his heart grew bitter over the loss of his Darina. He hardened his heart and ploughed on.

 He crossed over into Adnak but it was too warm and he once again turned north. Vigour was an embittered and angry man but he was finally satisfied when he reached a small town that rested on the Madyar border on The Bay of Glaciers. Summer was barred from any appearance in this northern community. Here Vigour thought he could live out his life in a frozen wasteland that matched his inner sentiment. The succour he had been searching for was not found so much in The Bay of Glaciers as it was in its climate. It was cold all of the time and this was Vigour's only consolation.

CHAPTER 9

LILY AND MOIRA were best friends. Moira worked at the pub and general trading post and Lily's father owned the establishment. Big Ben sold everything from ladies undergarments to snow shovels. If you wanted a nice mug of hot mead you would also head over to Ben's. Moira was a full figured red headed temptress while Lily inherited her mother's golden hair and spectral features. They were complete opposites but best of friends. Lily would often sneak Moira away to skate on the bay or to sled down the embankments. Big Ben never chastised the girls and was secretly happy that Lily had a companion with whom she could commune. He and Helga had expected to have several children but Lily was destined to remain an only child. Living in the far north without a friend would have been a very lonely existence. Moira was always there for Lily, to lend her friendship. The girls were both 16 years old but this remote destination offered little chance for a match for either of them. Ben was brewing a plan to send the girls south to live with relatives that could be trusted to make a good match for both young women.

Manfred, one of Ben's regular customers, was sitting on his regular stool at the end of the bar, mentally devouring Moira's ample curves, when Vigour entered Big Ben's for the first time. Manfred was instantly on alert; he could feel the power that Vigour kept tightly bound. Manfred's interest had not been piqued in many years and he vowed to get acquainted with this mysterious, scarred stranger. The temperature outside was well below the freezing mark and this newcomer had come into the bar wearing only a light broadcloth cape over summer weight hunting garb. Manfred sported a White bear coat with a hood to protect his ears when he ventured out into the elements. Strange. Vigour requested a cold brew rather than steaming mead and then he took a seat close to Manfred. The two exchanged looks and Manfred turned out to be a wealth of information that Vigour sought. Vigour explained that he hoped to settle in the area and he needed a place to stay until he decided where he could build a shelter of his own. Manfred was very pleased to offer Vigour a place at his lodge if he were willing to share in the hunting and the labour required to chop all the wood needed to heat the small cabin. Vigour readily agreed to the hunting and insisted that he would chop and carry all the wood in exchange for a place to stay for the meantime. Manfred startled Vigour when he suggested that Vigour might want to use his magic to fell the trees. Vigour had never had anyone speak to him in such a casual manner about magic. He had worked all of his life to hide his abilities. This man spoke about magic like it was a good thing. How had he even known that Vigour possessed any supernatural abilities?

Manfred had reason to hate the magicians that gathered in the south. They had excluded him, banished him, and his resentment had turned to hatred as he struggled to live in this hidden frozen backwoods. He was powerful and now he had found an apprentice who could probably rival and possibly surpass the abilities Manfred himself possessed. The best thing about this deformed man was the bitterness that lived in his heart. That emotion could be nurtured and turned into real hate. That is what Manfred had really been waiting for; a conspirator who could help him dole out the revenge that those virtuous southerners deserved. Manfred remembered when he had been next in line to become chancellor of The Society. He had access to all the libraries and all of the writings about the dark arts. He became obsessed with the possibilities. The dark arts offered a competent magician so much more than the White arts ever could. Manfred had only tried to mix a few potions, just to see if they worked, and for this transgression they had drummed him out. They told him that he had to leave the northern continent or he would face the wrath of the combined force of The Society. They escorted him to the Sonda, Cormer border and warned him not to return to the north or the consequence would be severe. In the end he had defied them. Manfred travelled through Crerar and along the southern coast of the Gulf of Kings all the way to Locan. There he crossed the straight by ferry and, like Vigour; he crossed the Borealis Mountains at the divide. From there he made his way north and finally settled in The Bay of Glaciers in the far north, just to spite his adversaries.

Manfred's cabin turned out to be more of a lodge. It was huge and luxurious. Vigour was more than surprised to find such an opulent dwelling in such a remote location. He soon discovered that Manfred had used magic to excavate and build this fortress. Below the frozen earth, there were catacombs leading to secret areas that could not be detected by common folk. Charms were cast around the lodge so that people who passed by saw only a simple cabin with smoke spewing from a crooked chimney. Manfred dropped the charm for Vigour; he did not plan to keep secrets from his new apprentice. Vigour's introduction to the dark arts was about to begin and Manfred planned to nurture the bitterness living in Vigour's heart into utter hatred.

Manfred and V spent almost every waking moment together. V enjoyed the power he wielded when he practiced the dark arts. It was like an addiction; the only thing better than power, was more power. His requisite for power fostered the growth of the seed of evil sprouting in his heart. The two soon realized that they would need more allies to be able to carry out the revenge that Manfred planned for the people of the south. Together, using the dark arts texts that Manfred had spirited away from the Society, they cast a crawler-web spell. Their insidious spell caused an invisible web to crawl along the earth in a number of random directions. The web passed through common folk causing them to shiver and nothing more. When the web encountered a gifted person, it would instill an overwhelming urge in that individual to travel north, toward The Bay of Glaciers.

Manfred and V sat drinking mead and brew at Ben's pub waiting for the gifted magicians to arrive. They arrived one by one and were welcomed to join the Enclave of Magic. Only a few candidates refused the offer and they were never heard from again. The enigma of the Enclave was paramount so the gifted arrivals either joined or died.

The following five years became an arduous and enlightening time for V. He spent hours pouring over the few texts that Manfred kept closely guarded in a special room that only he and V could enter. He learned to use his mind to conjure and control. In his unschooled state, V possessed dominion over fire, earth and water, he was a powerful practitioner. Now that Manfred had helped him to hone his skills, he felt that his potential was almost limitless. His only adversary was heat. He could not abide warmth and as he gained in power so his abhorrence for warmth increased. While indoors, he lived most of his days in a very cold and isolated area of the catacombs below the lodge. When he ventured outdoors, he needed little in the way of protective clothing because the icy climate was his domain. He always carried winter garb so that it could be donned just before he entered the town. His visits to Ben's were still frequent and V did not want to draw attention to his strange attributes.

One candidate who didn't actually arrive was a surprise to both Manfred and V. Moira approached them surreptitiously and suddenly opened her mind. They were stunned that Moira had been under their very noses all this time yet her skills were such that neither of them had been able to detect her.

Moira and V became soul mates. He trusted her enough to let her into his mind just as she had allowed him access to her own. They kept no barriers intact when they shared each other's thoughts thus they knew each other as well as they knew themselves. Moira was saddened to experience the way V viewed himself. The scars he still bore caused him to hate his own reflection. Moira also knew that V fancied Lily, Big Ben's daughter and her own best friend. Once Moira began spending most of her time at the lodge, she began researching ways to correct V's terrible face. Potions and salves all proved inadequate and some even caused the scars to appear worse by making them red and aggravated. Moira chose a new path. If she couldn't cause the scars to disappear from V's face, maybe she could make the scars disappear from people's minds. She fashioned an amber amulet and asked V to begin wearing it close to his skin. V held out little hope for banishing his scarred appearance but to placate his friend he wore the tiny amulet. Within weeks, the scars were noticeably diminished. After having worn the amulet for less than 6 months, V's face looked as it had before the fateful fire. It was an illusion, of course, and V was counselled to never remove the amulet because this would cause everyone to once again see what really lay below the impression of his new face. V was now ready to pursue Lily. Big Ben was thrilled because his daughter was now ready for marriage and this turn of events would keep her in the north, close to her parents who loved her more than life itself. Lily was overwhelmed and completely unprepared for this turn of events but she had always taken a shine to V, even before his face had healed. A bargain was struck and Lily became V's wife.

    The lodge, including its subterranean portion was no longer enough space to house the numerous magicians and sorcerers who answered the call of the web. In less than 5 years, the Enclave's numbers had multiplied several times. It was time to begin sending his minions to the south on fact finding missions so that a plan could be put in place to quench Manfred's thirst for revenge.

CHAPTER 10

V WAS IN CHARGE of the plans to move the Enclave to a secure location at North Point. This was the most northern place in Afshen that still received any natural light from the sun. It was situated at the tip of Afshen where the Northern Sea became the Bay of Ice. The only other habitable location was situated in the dark area of The Waste called Ice Port. Few people even ventured as far as North Point so this setting was selected to erect the Enclave, a castle large enough to shelter all the magicians who would answer the call to the north. V and Moira travelled there alone to put in place the charms that would ensure their privacy once they began constructing the planned edifice. It would be built entirely using magic. V had planned the elaborate design back at the lodge and felt ready and able to raise his planned structure manipulating the natural resources that were available in and around North Point.

The temperature at North Point had not risen above the freezing point in hundreds of years. The salty sea remained fluid but its waters were filled with bergs that showed only their apexes above the frosty surface. These floating behemoths were home to the mighty white bears of the northern continent. V stood on the frozen coast, littered with huge boulders, and surveyed the vista his new home would provide for many years to come. In the evening, huddled in their shelter constructed of thick animal hides, Moira and V sat in mental communion readying their combined powers for the work ahead. At the lodge, Moira had studied the texts that included much information related to the crafting of amulets and the drawing of power signatures. These signatures could be drawn using loose sand, salt or sawdust but they could also be burned into a surface using acids. When crafted correctly, these writings could multiply the powers of those magicians using them. Moira planned to use boiling oil to melt the signatures into the ice where the castle was to eventually stand. She guarded a small urn that protected the embers of the fire that she would soon need to heat her oil. V had the power to make fire burn, but he was unable to create fire without at least single ember to initiate a burning. Once he controlled a fire, he could cause anything to burn, even rocks and the earth itself. It was ironic that V had the power to control fire considering he had no tolerance for heat. There was very little in this vicinity that could be burned. Not a single tree or shrub grew anywhere on the north side of The Bay of Glaciers and North Point was situated a great deal further north of that location. V would certainly need to use all of his formidable powers to erect the castle he envisioned.

Moira religiously fed her ember with dried mosses and lichens to keep it alive and burning. She carefully set out a crucible which had a long handle and a tiny pouring spout. She placed it on a flat stone and fetched her precious ember. V was ready to begin. Concentrating on the embers smouldering safely in the urn, he caused the flat rock beneath the crucible to commence spewing forth scorching flames. While reciting a chant she had put to memory, Moira slowly poured the oil into the blistering crucible. The oil bubbled and gave off a pungent odour. It was time to begin the signature. Moira was in a trance while she chanted and poured the oil into intricate patterns on the frozen surface. V stood in the centre of the growing pattern dressed only in a loin cloth. The freezing temperature did not affect him, except to make him even more powerful. With the signature complete, from the periphery, Moira directed her own energy toward V. His entire body seemed to vibrate with a static charge that caused every hair on his body to stand erect. His feet left the ground and he floated, face down, above the elaborate signature with his arms spread to point to the north and to the south. From the north he gathered the powers of darkness with his right hand, and with his left hand, he tapped and fed upon the energy and the abundant life from the south. The ice and the very foundation of rock below V began to rumble and morph. Moira was thrown a great distance when the first rocks began to explode all around V's floating body. She remained unconscious for several hours while the earth shook and moved to organize itself according to V's will. When Moira finally regained her senses she was in awe of what her mentor had accomplished. The outlines of the castle were intact and somewhere inside, V continued to manipulate the elements to complete the mission he had orchestrated. At this moment, Moira understood that V was her master. Manfred's powers were nothing compared to this new quintessence of strength.

In less than a fortnight the stone castle, with its sweeping spires stood like a sentinel against the frozen coast. He had used all the power he could muster and he also tapped Moira when he felt the need. V was a truly formidable magician and Moira felt a fresh respect and a newly established fear for her old soul mate. The way she viewed V would, henceforth, be forever changed and laced with awe.

The Enclave was a frozen bastion which rivalled the palace in Manek for its sheer size. It was, however, nothing like the summery and decorative home of Zelebeth and Archer. Here in the north, V insisted on a minimalist environment where his minions would enjoy no comforts. The walls were bare and maintained the original finish of the grey and jagged boulders which had been used in their building. The hallways were dark and lined with frost because V did not allow heat inside his fortress. Not a single fireplace existed anywhere in this fortress. Cooking fires were not necessary because V had minions who could conjure all the food that would be necessary to feed his new subordinates. Manfred did not realize it yet but he was soon to be delegated to underling. V's new powers made him the new director of this horde of the dark arts.

The Enclave was now filled with his multitude, as V liked to call them. He had moved Lily to the castle but she was not very impressed with her new surroundings. Lily was fragile and suffered from the cold. Her twins seemed to thrive in the frigid surroundings, but Lily grew weak and sickly. Having Moira as her constant companion made the move away from her parent's home a little easier for Lily. Moira served as midwife when Lily gave birth to V's 2 set of twins. The boys, Kern and Zephyr, were born during the first year at the Enclave and the girls, Shandra and Frosh, arrived 2 years later. The children all showed signs of giftedness and would be properly schooled in the arts when they were of age.

V's minions were spread far and wide, settled into areas where they could gather information for their master. They used Northern Pigeons to stay in communication. The rookery at the top of the highest tower was the place where all messages arrived. Even the strongest telepaths could not communicate over such great distances. V's most trusted devotee, Carl, was able to garner an invitation to join The Society. Manfred's old nemesis, the chancellor, must be becoming very lax to allow Carl to infiltrate his domain; this was just the opportunity that Manfred had dreamed of. Unfortunately, he would not live to see his diabolical plans come to fruition.

Manfred forced a standoff with V when he discovered that members of the horde were taking secret directives from their newer and more powerful master, and thus he brought about his own downfall. It started as a heated argument but quickly escalated to using magic as a weapon. The two magicians cast spells at each other and it soon became evident that Manfred was no match for V. With his anger ignited, V threw all of his power into a conjuring that left Manfred totally incapacitated. V had changed Manfred into a white statue that stood moulded into the floor of the main hall of the castle directly above the powerful signature that still remained melted into the icy foundation of the castle. Manfred was not allowed to die. He would stare forever through eyes that would always remain open to take in the happenings at the Enclave. He would perpetually witness that V was in charge.

CHAPTER 11

LIFE ON THE farm, in Adnak, was happy and the winter had not been as harsh as many had feared. El was very busy with her three children. Mica was 4 and Nina was 2. Little Frederer was almost 1 and he was a handful. Jok was such an involved father that he was finding it arduous to leave the farm, even to take care of his trading concerns. Den agreed to accompany him on the trips so that he might learn the routes and eventually take over some of the responsibilities on his own. He was 15, after all, and he should begin helping Jok with the business. Fannie found it difficult when Den was away because she was so accustomed to sharing his mind. Den often attempted to remain in contact with Fannie when he and Jok left the farm, just to see over what distance he could still hear her thoughts. They did not realize this at the time but these attempts to remain in contact were actually helping them to hone their telepathic skills. Each time Den left the farm, the twins were able to read each other over greater and greater distances.

Fannie could still speak to Den as the wagon trundled over the bridge which led to the Southman gate in Manek. Inside, Jok skilfully made his way toward the pubs which purchased his products and once those deliveries were complete he parked the wagon at the market where people could either buy or trade for the remaining produce. It was after a trip just like this one, 6 years ago, that Jok had offered a ride to two waifs he found walking along the river road.

Jok left Den to sell the remains of their cargo while he made for the vendor who served the city's best meat pies. Mango and his wife had been baking these tasty pies since Jok began coming to the Southside market. Spiced apples were also one of their specialities and Jok always ate his fill at no charge since they were made from his apples. There was always a package wrapped for Jok to take home for the three little ones who anticipated the tasty treats upon their father's return.

Jok traded gossip with Mango who always seemed to know everything that was going on in the entire city. Today, Mango had some troublesome news for Jok. People had been in the market over the past three months asking questions about a set of twins that may be coming to do business in the selling zone. No one knew the twins because they had never both accompanied Jok on his city trips but Mango was a friend and he knew about Jok's children. After all this time, Jok considered Den and Fannie as much his own children as those he had with El. This news worried him and he wondered whether or not to tell Den. Mango suggested that Den should cover at least one of his eyes with a patch. It would not do for someone to take notice of his one violet and one green eye.

By the time Jok made his way back to the wagon with a patch that he had fashioned from some black broadcloth, Den was engaged in an animated conversation with a young girl. This was not the time to have him don his makeshift disguise, and as it happened, it was already too late. Archel was a novice from The Society. She had been chosen to approach the twins and to attempt to initiate them. The plan had been to communicate with Jok before speaking to Den and Fannie directly but as fate would have it, Den was alone at the wagon when Archel arrived. Archel was an empath and she could read people's feelings with ease. Her gift also engendered trust and individuals automatically believed and confided in her.

Archel was such an open and honest person that Den and Jok both agreed to meet with her that evening and discuss her proposal. Sitting in a corner booth in a quiet pub, Archel told Den that she was a special person, just like he was. Her gift allowed her to identify him. She knew a lot about magic and she wanted to tell him all about it. Magic was no longer something to hide. This city embraced magicians and even sought them out. Queen Zelebeth herself had proclaimed an open invitation to magic practitioners to come to her palace and work together for everyone's common good. Magicians, sorcerers and wizards were all being made welcome. The Society would be pleased to receive Den as a candidate. He would be educated and all of his needs would be provided for as well. As Den read Jok's worried thoughts, he confirmed that he was also very wary of this offer. No mention had been made of Fannie and Den decided to keep her existence quiet for the time being. Den agreed that he and Jok would come to the palace the following day to meet with this Society and then they would make a decision. Archel promised to send a cart runner for them in the morning and bade them farewell. She did not want to appear to be coercing Den to make a decision for fear that he may choose to decline The Society's offer. She was wise to not mention Den's sister. This would have made him nervous and caused him to wonder how The Society knew so much about him and his sister.

Jok and Den sat in the booth for a long while thinking about all that they had learned from Archel. Den had never made such a bold decision without consulting Fannie and he was unsure of himself without her counsel. He and Jok agreed that they would learn nothing unless they met with the people of The Society. Once they had more information, they could go home and seek Fannie's advice. Den had been identified so there would be no more hiding, in any case.

The cart runner arrived at the appointed time and Jok and Den settled themselves for a long ride. Neither of them had ever crossed the city before. Even Jok was fascinated at the sheer size of the place. The route the cart runner took was almost the same one that Carlotta had travelled upon her return from Jok's farm. She had come in during the evening but Den and Jok first saw the castle in the morning light. The black marble was as dark as night and the white and pink marble trim seemed to shimmer at the edges of the edifice to give it an unearthly quality. Jok and Den were both in awe and their amazement only increased as they drew closer. The grounds in front of the castle were larger in area than the town where Den had last lived. Once they passed through the main gate they had to catch their collective breath. The gardens here were teeming with every sort of flower and shrubbery, all meticulously cared for. Gardeners made their way from one area to another snipping, pruning and watering. There were a myriad of walkways wide enough for two horse drawn carts to ride abreast. The walkways themselves were hewn from some sort of white stone that looked as if it were wet even though it was completely dry. The flat stone was set together so skilfully that the cart never registered a bump. In the centre of the garden, a hedge taller than 3 men was planted to form a huge labyrinth. Jok thought that El and the children would love to get lost in the maze and spend the afternoon finding their way back out. The city was a wonder but this palace was simply wondrous.

The cart runner turned away from the castle and made for a stone archway that was decorated with sculptures of mythical creatures with their tales and wings intertwined. The archway was huge and opened onto a courtyard that was smaller but rivalled the palace's garden with its beauty. Fountains dotted the landscape and set in the centre of each of these fountains was a sculpture of a water creature which spewed water from its mouth. Frog, fish, dolphin, mermaid, even octopus all carved so carefully that they looked real and even seemed to move. The cart runner stopped in front of a large building which was also beautifully decorated. Every stone block used to build this structure was sculpted into a picture. The pictures were in an order that told a story. Den would have liked to stand in front of the building and read the picture story but Archel was walking out of the entry way to greet them. She paid the cart runner and directed him toward the comfort station where he could refresh himself, eat and nap until his services would again be required. She beckoned the men to follow her into the building.

Archel explained that they were currently inside the main hall of the welcoming plaza where entire delegations of visitors could be made comfortable. There were potted palms, vases of fresh cut flowers and cushioned chairs set close to lovely round marble tables. There were hundreds of alcoves circling the huge hall and inside each alcove stood a statue of a man or a woman sculpted to twice actual size. Each statue had a silver floor plaque explaining who the immortalized person had been. The room made Den's head spin. He had never witnessed such opulence. Today was a quiet day and they would be able to wander the grounds without being disturbed or distracted. Walking through the building on the main floor, they exited at the rear where there was an enormous courtyard surrounded by buildings even larger than the welcoming plaza. Archel pointed out the new candidate dorms where Den would live if he chose to come to The Society. The other buildings housed the chancellery, the apartments for the ruling members, the libraries, the baths and of course, the mess. Swimming pools were located inside each building and fresh water was pumped through each pool directly from either the river or the sea. The beach was located across the palace grounds and the candidates were welcomed to use it as they pleased. There were catacombs under the entire grounds where artifacts and magical ingredients could be safely stored. The Society employed hundreds of lay workers so the members and candidates had no chores or responsibilities. They need only concentrate on education and practicing their skills and gifts. Archel could see that Den was impressed. There is only one condition to joining The Society, but she would let the chancellor tell Den about that when they met.

The chancellor, Morgan Alfred-son, was an elderly gentleman with a friendly face and an abundant waistline. He was not the most gifted wizard at The Society but he was the founder and he had been one of King Gaylord's best friends. Morgan was the main reason that The Society was welcomed and nurtured at the palace in Manek.

His office had an exceptionally high ceiling that was dominated by a huge skylight. The walls were lined with pigeon holes that were stuffed and overflowing with documents and rolled parchments. His desk and tables were laden with books and papers, so much so, that no surface remained which was not beleaguered. After the pristine gardens and the opulent welcoming building, this office looked like a shambles to Den and Jok when they were escorted in to meet the chancellor. Morgan pushed his ample self out of his cushioned chair to make his way across the room to greet his guests. He was so happy to meet Jok but especially thrilled to finally be acquainted with Den. Morgan did not stand on ceremony and pumped Jok's hand vigorously and patted Den on the shoulder in greeting. He invited them to sit and immediately sent Archel to order refreshments. Jok could guess that by the look of him, this man enjoyed his repast often.

Rather than getting right down to business, Morgan chatted with Jok about this year's crops and the damage that may have been done the previous winter when the frost came early and refused to leave till well past its usual time. Jok aired confidence that the northern agricultural community had survived the strange cold much better than the southern continent. The plantings in the north were hardy and less apt to sustain permanent damage from a lengthy freeze. The southern plantings, especially the citrus trees, had been those which would never recover from the low temperatures they had endured. Pity, Morgan relished the abundant varieties of orange and yellow skinned fruits that arrived by ship from Cormer and The Blue Coast.

Archel returned and was followed by several young boys carrying trays laden with morsels of fancy tidbits. Each huge tray was laden with meat, fruit and a variety of cheeses with grain crisps. There were sauces for dipping the meats and sweet mixtures and dry sugars which could be used to coat the fruit. Morgan's refreshments could have fed Jok's entire family for days. The sugars were an exceptional treat since Jok's farm used only honey as their means to sweeten or can fruits. These powdery crystals were a wonder that neither Jok nor Den had ever tasted. Each tray bearer positioned himself next to Morgan and each of his guests because there was no cleared area to set the trays down. Jok and Den helped themselves to the feast and Morgan ate like he had been starved for a week.

Morgan was not the aristocrat that Jok and Den had expected. Instead his easy going manner and antics had set them at ease even in these daunting surroundings. Morgan spoke like a farmer, welcomed guests like a farmer and ate like a farmer. During their conversation, they learned that Morgan had actually been a farmer before he discovered his magical gifts. His fruit had been so succulent that the King had summoned him to supervise the planting of the palace orchards. That had been the beginning of a long and solid friendship between two men, one a lowly farmer and the other the King of the realm.

Morgan had never left the employ of the King and he had never married. The rest was history. The King's best friend used magic; so magic had to be accepted as good. The Society was an idea that the two men had hatched so that someone could ensure virtuousness and keep watch so that magic would always be used for the common good.

Jok and Den now knew the history of The Society and felt less anxious, greatly due to Morgan himself. So that he could be entirely sure of Morgan's intentions, Den sent out a tendril to probe Morgan's thoughts. A huge smile burst across Morgan's face and Den felt himself pulled into the jolly man's mind. This was a different experience for Den; he was not the one controlling the exchange and although he was initially disconcerted, he readily relaxed and exchanged thoughts and memories with the old man. Den detected no malice in Morgan. He would be able to share this entire episode with Fannie when he linked with her back at the farm.

The entire exchange lasted only a few brief seconds and when the men broke their link, they were both smiling. Den believed that he had found his destiny. This was where he and his sister belonged. Here they would not be hiding their abilities nor would they be worrying about putting those who cared for them at risk. Den was sure that Fannie would agree to come and live with The Society. Morgan needed to meet with Fannie and link with her before any formal invitation could be garnered but he felt secure that all would proceed without complication. His face grew serious as he warned Den about the one and only rule that governed all the members and candidates at The Society. It was forbidden to use magic for any greedy or evil ends. This transgression would result in expulsion or even death. Den understood the gravity of Morgan's warning but neither he nor Fannie had ever tried to use magic except to lessen suffering or to curb some disastrous event. Of course, Morgan already knew this because he had shared Den's thoughts and memories so he was well aware of each situation when the twins had used their unschooled powers. Fate had brought Den to meet his destiny; he just needed to convince his sister to join him.

CHAPTER 12

JOK AND DEN were well fed and provided with comfortable lodging for the night. Their shared bedroom, with formidable double doors, was twice as large as the kitchen back at the farm. Here, the windows were covered with glass that could be pushed aside to let the cool sea breeze flow in. The furniture was all crafted from rich hardwoods with delicate marble inlays which were set in artistic designs. Exquisite hangings decorated the walls and silken fabric enclosed each of the beds. Even the floor was covered with rich wool carpets that had been crafted by artisans and depicted images of animals, the likes of which Jok had never known. A guide was assigned to help the men find their way as they explored the grounds and gardens. They actually swam in a pool where the salty sea water refreshed and exhilarated them. By the time they were ready for sleep, both Jok and Den were so physically tired, neither could appreciate the feather beds they rested upon.

The next day dawned and it was time for Jok and Den to leave this opulence and once again enter the world to which they were accustomed. They bade farewell to Morgan with a promise to return with Fannie very soon. Morgan instructed them to hire a cart runner upon their return to Manek and to give him a small red card that he handed Den. The Society would bear the expense and refresh the runner when he deposited them at the palace. They said their final farewells and followed Archel to the gates where she arranged for a fresh cart runner to deposit the men back at the pub's stable where they had boarded the horses.

As the cart runner weaved them through the busy city, Jok and Den were able to pay closer attention and admire more of the grandeur and diversity around them. Entire sections of the city were populated with people whose heritage Jok could not guess. They seemed to live in specific areas but they all worked together. Short people with a yellow cast complexion crowded a large neighbourhood where the spicy food smells were enticing even to Jok and Den, who had bellies still brimming with breakfast. As they passed through another of the city's numerous gates they focused on people with ebony skin who were tall and stately. Everybody seemed to be engaged in some fashion of work. People hurried to appointments or tended their shops as Den and Jok made their way further and further away from the centre of this complex city. So many cultures coexisted and worked side by side to meet the needs that made this machine of a city run to its full capacity. The cart runner dropped them by the pub entrance and was on his way for a well deserved rest.

It was only just past the noon hour so the men harnessed the horses and headed out of the city. Jok stopped at Mango's to get some food for their journey and soon they were crossing the stone bridge heading west along the river road. They regaled their exciting day as they made their way home to El, the children and Fannie.

They made good time because the road was almost deserted. Den was as anxious to arrive home as Jok was and they estimated that they could get there before the children were tucked in their beds. Den had so much to think about on his way home that it hadn't even occurred to him that he hadn't tried to contact Fannie to let her know that they would be arriving that evening. As Jok turned the tired horses into the long laneway, he had no idea what had taken place on his farm just a few short hours ago.

It was early in the morning and El was bathing Frederer at the kitchen sideboard where she had a good view of the laneway. Fannie was entertaining Mica and Nina while preparing vegetables for the midday meal soup pot that hung over the hearth in the fireplace. With her mind link, Fannie could see what El saw at the end of the lane. Several men on horseback had stopped and were surveying the farm and the area thereabouts. A covered wagon came around the bend and was waved onto the laneway which lead to the farmhouse. Company was on its way.

Fannie and the two older children stepped out onto the porch to greet the visitors who arrived just as El came out carrying Frederer wrapped in a towel, his hair still dripping. Fannie's senses were warning her that these men posed some kind of danger but she stood her ground and greeted them cordially. She didn't want the men to see fear so she chose to appear smug as though the men of the family were somewhere close by. Three of the men got off their horses and approached the family group on the porch. They wanted to know where they could find a set of twins who should be around the age of 15 or 16 years. They would give no information or reason for the enquiry but they said that they knew the twins were reported to live at this farm. The names of the twins they were searching for were Den and Fannie.

Fannie was inwardly frantic. What did these men want with her and Den? How did they know where to find her? How did they know their names? What should she do? Questions bounced back and forth between El and Fannie as they faced the threatening group on their property. El warned Fannie to tell the men nothing. El was afraid for the children and as it came to pass, she had good reason to be terrified of these men. Fannie did the only thing she could think of. She cast her mind out to find Den if he were within her range. She and El were in trouble, they needed help. She tried to warn him of the situation which was playing itself out at the farm. At that very moment, Den was with Jok eating a sumptuous breakfast in The Society's mess. It would not be till noon that Den would be in range for a conversation with his sister and by then it would be much, much too late.

These men were rugged looking and they appeared to have been travelling for days. Their dark clothing was covered with road dust and the horses looked thirsty and tired. They had little patience for these women who had not uttered a word since they had questioned them about the twins. The three men who were on their feet approached the porch and leaned provocatively on the banister. They appraised El and then turned all of their attention to Fannie. If they had meant to intimidate the women, they had succeeded. A cold sweat broke out on Fannie's forehead and she was close to panic.

A small commotion began near the covered wagon which had stopped by the barn. A small man wearing black clothing and a long black cape came strolling around the wagon and toward the house. His hair was combed back and held at the nape of his neck with a leather thong. His black eyes were so dark that they seemed like pools of gloom. As he approached the porch, he smiled and his demeanour suggested that he was a man who got what he asked for. His first words warned the women that if they chose to defy him, they would regret that decision. He gave two of the dusty men at the rail a nod to approach El. They closed in on her and threatened her with their proximity. Fannie moved to put herself between El and the men but one of the goons grabbed her arm and turned her to face the man in black. He threatened that this was his final warning. If they elected to keep the information he needed from him, the children would be the first to suffer. The other dusty hooligan on the porch moved swiftly and grabbed Frederer out of El's arms and held him by the ankle and dangled him over the rail. If El had a voice, everybody would have heard her scream. Instead, Fannie was the only one who could hear the scream that only a mother could wield when her child is threatened. Mica wailed with fear and Nina stood mute in shock. As this tragedy unfolded, the other men who had remained on their horses up till this time dismounted and made their way into the barn. Moments later, the farm animals were loosed from the barn and scurrying in every direction. The sheep were easily startled and made for the pasture at a run. The cows walked and the horses ran toward the orchard. The sow and her brood were the last to be shooed out of the barn and they were in no hurry to go anywhere. The chickens were frantically running in circles causing themselves more panic than need be.

Amid the chaos, Frederer's screams were loudest as he protested his situation. The man in black gave a silent order and the men near the barn began killing the piglets in the yard. Their knives were swift and blood spurted as the angry sow charged anyone she could see, as her brood died. The evil leader of this motley band was laughing out loud as he witnessed the carnage. He promised that the youngest child would be next.

Fannie gave him the information he wanted. She was the twin he was seeking. She closed her mind tightly so that even El could no longer hear her. Fannie admitted that she and her brother were the ones he was looking for but it was too late to find them both. She told the man in black that her brother was dead.

The malevolent man strolled up onto the porch and looked closely at Fannie. He walked around her as she stood shaking with fear. He reached toward her face and let his hand drop to her slender neck where he jabbed her with a pointed instrument he held hidden in his hand. The elixir on the sharp, needle-like, implement caused Fannie to lose consciousness within seconds. She dropped to the porch and El ran to help her.

The caped man grabbed El and forced her to look into his eyes. He began questioning her but she was unable to respond. She tried to communicate her disability but that only angered the man further till he pushed her into the doorway where she hit her head hard enough to fall unconscious into the kitchen. The dusty man dropped Frederer and he suffered a broken arm and lay naked and wailing by the porch. Nina and Mica were bound together and tied to the porch rail so that they could not run for help or raise an alarm.

Fannie was unceremoniously loaded into the covered wagon where she was securely bound and gagged. The man in black looked smug as he stepped up and into the darkened wagon and the horsemen made ready to leave the farm. In less than the time it had taken Fannie to prepare the vegetables earlier that morning, life had changed for everyone in Jok's family, especially for Fannie.

CHAPTER 13

E L WAS STILL unconscious in the kitchen doorway when Jok and Den turned down the laneway that evening. The children were still tied to the porch rail but their voices were used up. They had cried and called for their mother all day and by this time neither of them could even utter a squeak. Frederer had managed to crawl up the stairs and nestle himself against his mother's prone body while his arm rested across her chest at an odd angle. There was still enough light for Den and Jok to see that something was amiss. They were not yet close enough to see the piglets lying in pools of blood in the front yard but they did notice that many of the animals were loose and untended. Den immediately tried to contact Fannie but she was not here. How could this be? Fannie never left the farm.

Den jumped from the wagon and all his senses were on alert. He ran at his best speed toward the house where he was the first to see the devastation. Jok tried to hurry the horses but they were too slow so he just jumped and ran after Den. Den was already on the porch untying the children when Jok arrived. The blood and the dead piglets in the yard had shocked Jok as he ran to his home. He saw his El on the floor just inside the doorway. Den came in behind Jok, carrying Mica and Nina, trying to calm them. He set them down beside their mother as Jok cradled El in his arms. Frederer screamed when he was moved and Den saw that his arm was injured, probably broken. Jok carried El to the sleeping area where he laid her gently on the straw mattress. He could find no injury that required tending, only a large bump on her head, so he and Den concentrated their efforts on little Frederer. El would wake on her own . . . . or she wouldn't; Jok didn't even want to entertain that idea.

Where was Fannie? Den was becoming frantic but Frederer had to come first. If Fannie had been anywhere close by, the children would not have been left tied up and Frederer would have been tended to. He could not find her with his mind so that left him with three choices: she was so far away that she couldn't hear his mind, she was unconscious somewhere, like El, or she was dead. He could not face the last choice so he would have to search for her once everybody here was taken care of.

Jok and Den organized themselves. Den bundled an angry Frederer and left the house. He turned the horses that were still hitched to the wagon and with a tightly wrapped Frederer; he made his way to the healing woman's home a short distance to the north. She would be able to set his little arm back into place and provide some type of healing potion for his pain. She could prepare a poultice for El's injury and Den would bring it back with him as quickly as possible. Meanwhile, Jok stayed at home to comfort his traumatized children and wait for his El to waken from her healing sleep. He left them for only a few moments to keep his promise to Den. He searched the barn and the immediate area to see if Fannie was lying unconscious in need of help. He would have bad news for Den when he returned with Frederer. Jok wondered if El would be able to tell him what had happened here when she woke . . . if she woke. Without Fannie, how would he and Den communicate with El? Nina had barely acknowledged him since he arrived home. She suffered some kind of shock and it could take days for her to recover. Mica was his best hope to learn what had transpired and why his family had been targeted but he had no voice as of yet and Jok did not want to coerce the child, not tonight. Some of his animals had been killed, his wife and children had been hurt and Fannie was nowhere to be found but nothing had been stolen so what motive had there been to commit this atrocity?

CHAPTER 14

EL REMAINED UNCONSCIOUS for two full days. During this time, Den conducted another thorough search for Fannie. She was no longer on the farm; at least he did not find her body. When El finally woke, she was groggy and unable to leave her bed for an additional day. Once she drank some broth and nibbled some bread crisps her strength began to return. She was very frustrated with her inability to communicate. With her eyes, she pleaded with Mica to relate the events of that fateful day to his father. Jok was a patient father and did not relish having his young son relive the horrible morning but he needed to know what had happened. Den tried to read Mica and El but he was unable to form a connection. Nina remained completely uncommunicative and El silently worried for her little girl, who cuddled close to her mother and stared wide eyed into nothingness.

The following morning, Mica looked at his father and told him that it had started at this time of the day. He spent an hour relating the entire spectacle in the order it had all occurred. El cried silent tears when Mica told of Fannie's courage and how she tried to stand up to the men who were threatening the family. Mica related how Fannie had given herself up to the brigands when little Frederer had been endangered. El nodded her agreement with Mica's retelling to confirm that his story was correct. Nina stared into oblivion and Frederer slept throughout the horrific telling. Den listened carefully and steeled himself for what he knew he had to do. His mission was clear; he had to find his sister. He had an advantage. Whoever was searching for him thought he was dead. He planned to leave tomorrow but as of yet, he had no idea where to look.

El sat and watched as Jok and Den sombrely debated late into the night. Jok couldn't leave his family to help Den search for Fannie. He had no advice to help Den decide where to search for his sweet sister until he finally concluded that only one course of action made any sense; Den should go to The Society and enlist their help. Jok truly believed that this was Den's best hope of finding Fannie. Jok and El loved Fannie almost as much as Den did and they wanted nothing more than to have the twins back and safe.

It was a couple of days before Den could foresee leaving the farm. The animals were settled but the chores would be too much for Jok while he struggled to nurture his children and his wife back to a semblance of normalcy. El was saddened with her inability to communicate, Nina still uttered only one word sentences and Frederer was healing but still afraid of being held by anybody. Mica fared best, having dealt with his trauma during the telling. Somehow he'd accepted the brutality that he had witnessed and locked it tightly away where it would not constantly dominate his thoughts. Jok was being pulled in several directions and was often scattered and unable to finish any job that he started. Fate had dealt Jok's family a severe blow and they would need time to heal.

The days passed slowly and on the third evening, Jok sat Den down on the porch and confided that although he wanted him to stay at the farm, he knew that time was wasting and Den needed to be on his way. It was a full day's journey to Manek on horseback and that was what Jok intended to provide for Den. The chestnut mare would be his and she would serve him well on his quest to find his sister. Den had delivered the tiny foal and he had named her Dash when she was several weeks old because she was in a hurry to go everywhere. Jok wanted Den to leave the following day because he knew that time was of the essence. Den agreed and the day was set. El packed the saddlebag with dried fruits that wouldn't spoil so that Den could ride straight through to Manek without delay. Jok pulled a wooden box from under his sleeping pallet and counted out 3 silver slivers and 30 copper coins. This was all that he could spare but Den was hesitant to accept such a generous offering. Jok insisted that he might find himself in a circumstance where he would need some coin so Den graciously accepted. Plans for his departure were set and all Den needed now was a sound sleep so that he would be fresh for the long ride. As dawn broke, El and Jok stood arm in arm on the front porch and watched as Den rode away.

CHAPTER 15

FANNIE WOKE UP very cold, lying on a large animal skin on the floor of the dark wagon as it rumbled over uneven terrain. She had no clue as to where she was, where she was headed, or why these people wanted her. Her first instinct was to attempt a link with Den but she caught herself before she opened her mind. Even while she had lain unconscious, her mind had remained sealed. It would not do to open her thoughts when her captors might have the powers to enter her mind. Den couldn't help her; Fannie had to work her own way through whatever fate had planned. Fannie struggled to focus and think clearly. She must have been drugged by that evil man in black. She wondered how much time had passed since the horrible episode at the farm. She worried for El's and the childrens' safety. Had the ghastly men left El's family alone after Fannie confessed her identity or had they been killed? What did Den and Jok find when they arrived home from Manek? She had too many questions and just as many possibilities. The only thing that she was sure of was that Den would come to find her; at least he would try. About this, she was absolutely positive.

Fannie could hear the horses trotting alongside the wagon and she surreptitiously used her tingling fingers to investigate the bindings that were keeping her wrists securely bound behind her back. They had used leather thongs to tie her up. Her ankles were also tied securely so her movements were very restricted. Although it was dark inside the wagon, she lay on her side so she could see well enough to observe that it was furnished with a sleeping pallet and a small table and bench which were all fastened to the floor. Bolted to the floor in the middle of the wagon stood a beye'shtok, a freestanding potbellied stove that thankfully radiated heat. She believed that her captors would eventually come to check on her so if she could plan an escape, this was the optimum time.

Fannie fussed with the leather thongs but they must have been dampened before they were used because they had dried and tightened to the point of causing her circulation to almost stop. This explained the tingling in her fingers. Before she had time to work on the dried knots, the man in black made his way into the back of the wagon. He must have been sitting with the driver but he was here now, looking into Fannie's special eyes.

He introduced himself as Jeeree and smiled widely. He engendered fear. Fannie decided at that moment that she would not cooperate with this repulsive man. He surprised Fannie by not expecting any cooperation only her obedience. He offered to release her from her bindings and to provide her with some warmer clothing if she promised not to attempt an escape. Fannie viewed this as an opportunity. After all, what did she have to lose? She owed his man no allegiance. She glared at Jeeree as he used his knife to cut her free. He intimidated her further as he explained that she was currently a great distance to the north and she would find herself in a frozen wasteland when she arrived at her destination. He was being honest with her as he went on to explain that she had remained unconscious for more than 3 days. The heat from the beye'shtok was all that kept her from freezing. They had travelled without stopping to rest and had crossed the Adnak border into Kandar early yesterday. They would reach the Afshen border within the next 2 to 3 days, depending on the weather. From where The Bay of Glaciers dipped into Afshen, they would travel by dogsled to reach North Point, located 12 more days travel to the north.

Fannie's head was spinning. How would Den ever guess to search for her in this remote wasteland? She demanded to know why she had been taken from her home. Jeeree refused to answer any of her questions but he promised that very soon someone would be very pleased to enlighten her. The way he said it, made Fannie squirm with revulsion; who could be worse than this black clad monster?

Fannie's plans for escape were quashed by the climate. There was no place to run even if she could get away from her keepers. The ground was covered with snow, something that she had heard tell of but never seen. She and Den had seen the frost that clung to the blades of grass early in the mornings, before the sun melted it. They had endured a harsh winter at Jok's farm but harsh did not include snow in Adnak. Frosty temperatures and cold winds were the worst that Fannie had ever endured. The wagon's wheels had been exchanged for long rails that kept the wagon riding high over the snowy surface. The horses wore blankets to keep them safe from the punishing winds. Fannie was wrapped tightly in a coat fashioned from the hide of an animal, its fur still intact. Jeeree provided her with hand coverings and warm boots that wrapped each of her legs to just below her knees. These were all lined with plush fur that kept her tiny feet and fragile fingers from freezing. Fannie supposed that wherever she ended up she would be looked after. All the care she was receiving led her to believe that she was valuable to somebody important.

She began to speculate as the leagues slowly passed. Fiona and Lars were her adoptive parents. Could this be one of her real parents seeking her out after all of these years? If that were so, the men would not have threatened to hurt El or the children . . . unless her parents were evil. She had to stop this lackadaisical guesswork, it threatened her sanity.

Fannie was lightly drugged and roughly led into an inn where the group took on fresh supplies and spent the night in warm rooms. Hot chai was served in the morning just before the group once again resumed their arduous journey. After travelling for several more days, they arrived at Bluff Bay, where the group sheltered themselves and ate hot food in a tiny lodge occupied by a couple who kept dogs and apparently enjoyed life in these adverse conditions. They spoke a language that Fannie could not fathom so communication was not an option with these shy people. Their tan complexions and flat eyes gave them the same look as the animals which frolicked in the waters of the bay that Fannie could see out her window. They looked like happy monsters which emerged from the sea to play with each other on the frozen coast. What magic kept these creatures from freezing solid out in the bitter cold? Fannie decided that this remote place held wonders as well as peril.

Eight dogsleds were readied for the band of travellers. Fannie was bundled up and deposited on a sled which also carried some gear. Jeeree stepped onto the back of the sled and used a whip to urge the dogs to pull. The other sleds followed Jeeree's, as he forced the dogs further and further north. He had told her the truth so far. They were following the route he had described to her on her first day of consciousness in the covered wagon. If she remembered correctly, it would be days before they arrived at their intended destination.

They stopped each night to rest and feed the dogs. When they required sleep, the men built shelters using the very snow they travelled upon. They cut blocks of icy white snow with which they fashioned structures that, once completed appeared as white eggs stuck half way into the surface. They crafted a short passageway below the snowy facade that led inside the structure. Somehow, heat remained trapped inside the domed construction which provided an excellent shelter from the elements outside.

In the evening of her 12th day on the sled, Fannie caught sight of a black obelisk on the horizon. The dogs picked up speed as they spied their destination which promised food and rest. As they drew closer, it looked like a castle but it wasn't black, after all. It was the colour of an old boulder that sat by a road and gathered dust and white moss. The castle was actually coated with salt that had been deposited on its surface by the spray from the breaking waves on the rocky coast. Once they had passed through the gates, Jeeree formally welcome Fannie to the Enclave.

CHAPTER 16

FANNIE FOLLOWED JEEREE up the sweeping staircase into a huge room that was cavernous and furnished with only a few pieces. Those furnishings were made of the same material as the castle walls. Everything in this Enclave seemed to be made from stone. The seats were covered with animal pelts, probably to make them more comfortable or so that the seated individual wouldn't feel the cold that seemed to radiate from everything in the castle. Fannie had expected to remove her outerwear once inside the castle but her frosty breaths warned her that she would need to stay well bundled during her imprisonment at the Enclave. Wall sconces burned at spaced intervals in the walls but the fires were kept low and a minimum of heat was generated. This was becoming more and more peculiar by the moment. Jeeree sat down and relaxed as though he expected to wait a considerable time. Fannie tucked her legs up under herself and curled up on the fur covered, rock hewn settee and dozed. At least the wind was not blowing into her face and although it was terribly cold it felt balmy compared to the outdoors where Fannie had spent the last several days.

Fannie was wakened by a server who offered her warm chai and pieces of buttered bread with cheese. She hadn't realized how ravenous she was. Twelve days of fish rations had left her with a new reverence for bread and cheese. The hot tea warmed her till she thought that the feeling in her fingertips was actually returning. Sometime while she slept, Jeeree had left the room and once the server made his exit, Fannie was alone. The large entranceway was wide open and Fannie ate her repast as she walked around the echoing room. Her kidnapper was making a point . . . there was nowhere to run. Fannie knew escape was futile. She resumed her seat and waited for whatever was to come.

Moira glided into the room some time later. She appraised Fannie with her amber eyes and then came to sit next to her. She whispered a warning, advising Fannie to be on her best behaviour when the master made his imminent appearance. Fannie determined that she had been left waiting long enough to make her anxious and worried. It was time to get some answers to the questions she had been asking since the day of her abduction.

V walked into the room like a man who had a mission. He did not flaunt his power over Fannie the way Jeeree had done, he simply exuded command. He extended his apologies for the trip he had forced upon her but he promised that it had been for her own good. He promised that everything would soon be revealed; all her questions would be answered after she rested and felt more at home. He sat beside Fannie and held her hand in both of his as he delivered sympathies for her loss. It took Fannie a moment to realize that he was talking about Den. Just thinking of her twin warmed her heart, even in this frozen palace. V was not at all what Fannie had expected. He bade Moira show Fannie to her living quarters in the upper reaches of the Enclave.

Her room was much like the rest to the Enclave. It was cold, grey, and furnished with a bed, chair and table made of frozen drab rock. The only warmth to be found was the food and the spicy chai neither of which stayed hot very long.

CHAPTER 17

ON THE FIRST morning of her captivity, Fannie made her way down the stairs toward a room where she heard quiet conversation. She peeked around the archway and saw several groups of people, young and old, sitting around tables much like the one in her room. There were no sounds coming from any other direction so she decided to join the assemblage and see what she could learn about this place. She wondered if all these people could be captives just like she was. Fannie settled her nerves and walked as calmly into the room as she could. A few heads turned to look at her but she did not raise an undue interest so she scanned the room till she saw a vacant seat and headed in that direction. Like every room in the Enclave, this one was cavernous, grey and above all, cold. Everyone was bundled in warm wear but they all seemed content and engaged in animated conversation within their separate groups. She kept her eyes downcast and sat demurely on an oversized granite chair. She didn't know what to say so she sat, mute, waiting to hear what the 2 boys sitting at this table would talk about.

A towering boy, with skin the colour of a dried apple ring, surveyed Fannie with interest and immediately stood to welcome her. He bowed deeply and with a warm smile he addressed Fannie. He assumed she was a new arrival and in need of someone to show her around. His name was Shilinar B'Edard and he explained that he had journeyed from Locan, on the Southern Continent. He laughed out loud when he mused about the climate that he so sorely missed. He had lived at the Enclave for several months and was quite familiar with the layout of the areas open to candidates. Fannie told the boys her name and reasoned that she should pose as a candidate, whatever that entailed. The other boy, a rotund, jolly and very black fellow, was named Mushookoalah and he had travelled all the way from the city of Yama located on the coast of The Gulf of Plenty in the Inland Sea. He also mourned his sunny and sultry climate. He had arrived only 10 days ago and was still making himself familiar with the castle. He suggested that they explore together, with Shilinar as their guide. From the way they spoke, Fannie determined that these boys had travelled north of their own accords. Perhaps she could learn why they had come here and why she had been brought here.

    Servers soon arrived and doled out hot food and chai for the candidates to break their fasts. With their hungers satisfied, many of the candidates made their ways out of the dining hall and Fannie and the boys set out to explore the Enclave. Shilinar led the way and in no time at all, Fannie was so turned around that she feared that she would never find her way back on her own. This castle was a labyrinth of dimly lit hallways that opened onto rooms that were too numerous to count. Some rooms were occupied by groups of people reading books or listening to lecturers. Other deserted areas stood empty and bleak. Overall, Fannie found the Enclave depressing and desolate. Shilinar guided his small group up a winding stairway that was completely unlit; none of the sconces were burning. The only rays of light that entered this upward passage came from long slits in the outer wall which also let in the winds that battered the outside of the castle. Fannie guessed that they were making their way up one of the towers that she had briefly seen while sledding toward the Enclave. The climb was gruelling but Shilinar promised that the view from the top would compensate them for all their efforts. They finally emerged on a rocky platform at the top of the tower. In the centre of the circular area stood a podium which held a statue of a beautiful woman holding her arm out toward the south east. All three stood, mesmerized by her magnificence, and paid homage to the woman who must have posed for this masterpiece. She was so artfully crafted that she appeared surreal; her eyes seemed to emanate sadness and her hair seemed to actually be blowing away from her face in the strong winds. As one, the explorers turned to face in the direction she pointed. Shilinar explained that this was the Bay of Ice, which eventually led inland to become The Bay of Glaciers. Across the bay lay a land called The Waste where only a few hearty whale hunters maintained an encampment at Ice Port, where they slaughtered the huge beasts and froze the fat and tender meat for trade. Once he had seen a heavy ice barge rounding North Point, turning to make its way south, between the dangerous floating bergs, to trade bounty for goods and services in The Port of Merle. Fannie leaned close to the edge of the tower and peered down the sheer wall that ended in the snow and rocks of the coastline. The animals which frolicked in the surf looked like no more than dark dots from this altitude. When she turned around, she was dizzy and light-headed. V chose this moment to make his presence known. He glided slowly around the statue which had hidden him from view up until this time. The boys both bowed and kept their eyes averted when they recognized the master. V dismissed the boys with a wave of his hand; both Shilinar and Mushookoalah made for the stairway that would take them back into the Enclave.

V made eye contact with Fannie and probed the edges of her mind. Her defences were up and he laughed when he was unable to unlock her privacy barriers. He would remain content to talk with Fannie. He once again welcomed her to his abode and seemed quite sincere when he apologized for her kidnapping. The thugs who had been sent to retrieve her had misunderstood his instructions. They were meant to treat her kindly and to protect her from harm, not harm her as they had. V assured her that Jeeree and his men would face the consequences of their actions. Fannie was becoming more relaxed but she remained alert and cautious nonetheless. V needed Fannie to trust him before he could begin her education. It would not be wise to school an apprentice who had the potential to outshine her master. Manfred had made just such an error and he had paid for his mistake. V's old master continued to remain captive inside the statue which was the singular adornment in the main hall of The Enclave.

V assured Fannie that she was brought to the castle in the north to protect her from those individuals who abhorred magic. Fannie was well aware that such people existed; in fact she had spent most of her young life concealing her skills to avoid persecution. This place would be her refuge, V assured her. Here she would be free to explore her gifts and to learn how to increase her powers. All of his explanations seemed viable and Fannie found herself wondering if this was such a bad place, after all. She chatted with V for most of the morning and eventually accepted her circumstances. Obviously, there was nowhere to run and most of the people she had encountered at this Enclave appeared to be here of their own accords. She would let time judge V by his own actions. The one thing she knew with certainty was that she would not share the truth about the existence of her brother, not with anybody.

CHAPTER 18

V AND MOIRA LAY together in their feather bed, discussing Den and Fannie. Moira had recently replaced Lily as V's favourite. She had magical powers and the children she might one day give him would be more powerful than the two sets of twins that Lily had birthed.

Lily had grown weary of the cold and constantly begged to be allowed to go back to The Bay of Glaciers and let the children visit with their grandparents. She needed to see Big Ben and to stay at the inn that was warm and comfortable. V may have permitted Lily a visit with her parents but he would never consent to his children leaving The Enclave, even in the care of their own mother. Lily began to feel like more of a prisoner than the mistress of this castle. She grew depressed and then angry with her situation. At every opportunity she harangued and nagged V to let her make the trip that she so desired. Having made no headway with her stubborn husband, Lily made secret plans to make off with the children on her own. Her mistake had been in trusting her long time friend, Moira. V became enraged with Lily when he learned of her personal crusade. When he confronted her she had been outside on the platform at the top of the tower, staring in the direction where her parents lived. They quarrelled bitterly and V had finally endured all the disrespect he could deal with. As she stood pointing toward her old home, V's patience evaporated and rage took its place; he directed a static bolt at Lily which shrouded her and instantly began to form itself around her fragile body. Every hair on her head and every fibre of the fur garment she wore were frozen as if in a moment of time. The sadness captured in her expressions belied her thoughts; she would never see her children or her family again. No artisan could have created such a perfect work. She was immortalized on that podium where she still stood with her arm extended in the direction where her life was once happy. Like his old mentor, V's wife would remain locked inside a magical statue forever.

Moira bundled herself in a feather quilt while V lay sprawled on the bare rock surface of the bed. She sat cross legged while they chatted and discussed their plans. Fannie would come to trust V in time, Moira was sure of it. They had to give her time to digest the information she was being given and she may eventually tell them about her brother. V knew that Den was alive. He had received a pigeon only days after Fannie had been captured. His Society spy, Carl, had penned him a long message. Den was being broached by The Society. If things went as planned, it would not be very long before Den was led north to join his sister in V's hideaway. Jeeree's arrival at the farm to procure the twins, while Den was away, was just unfortunate timing. Instead of having both twins in his clutches, he only had Fannie. V intended for Den to find her and he would make sure that Carl helped. V was one of a select group who knew who these twins really were. He needed them on his side in the war that he anticipated. Left to The Society, they could swing the balance of power away from him. He had spent a lot of time and resources to locate the elusive twins; he intended to have them both.

CHAPTER 19

SIXTEEN YEARS AGO King Gaylord paced his enormous dining hall waiting to hear if his Queen had delivered him a boy or a girl child. The Queen was adamant that she be left alone with only her midwife for the delivery and thus everyone was barred from her private chamber. The midwife had an assistant who was mute and almost blind; the Queen allowed her to stay and provide the hot water and linens that were necessary. The midwife struggled to help the first child emerge. The boy was followed by his sister. Twins ran in the Queen's family. They were both fit and healthy. When the Queen looked into the eyes of her newborn children, her demeanour changed. She gathered her strength and stubbornly clutched the midwife as she gave instructions. These children were evil and could not be allowed to survive. Queen D'Enfanel recognised magic when she saw it. Each twin had one green and one violet eye; her sisters had had these strange eyes. Her parents had tried to raise the twin girls but no one could control their behaviour or the magical gifts they possessed. Eventually they were banished to live out their lives on one of the Crescent Islands far in the south.

D'Enfanel hated magic with a passion and her King must never be allowed to learn of what she was about to do. She wanted the twins drowned in the sea but she had to show her King a child. With clear instructions, the midwife made her way out of the castle using a surreptitious exit and ran to meet with some other midwives of her acquaintance. She needed a recently stillborn child that could be presented to the King as his own stillborn son. D'Enfanel had placed 2 gold sovereigns into the midwife's hand before she left the castle. One would pay for the child she would procure and the other would ensure her silence about the truth of what had occurred in these sealed chambers. As fate would have it, a child was available to the midwife and she re-entered the castle secretly, carrying the morbid bundle. The mute and nearly blind assistant, named Marva, was sent out of the chamber carrying a basket filled with soiled linens and concealing two very sleepy newborn children. Her instructions were to drown the twins in the sea and then to dispose of their little bodies so that no one would ever suspect that there had been any foul play. Another gold coin exchanged hands and the assistant, Marva, was sent along to perform her hideous duty. The midwife remained with the Queen to deliver the sad news to the anxious King.

Marva fully intended to carry out her macabre orders. She had never been in possession of anything as valuable as the gold sovereign that the Queen had pressed into her hand. As she made her way far down the beach to ensure that she was not seen, the children began to cry. Her heart was softened by the pleading sounds emerging from under the linen in her laundry basket. Before she could change her mind, she made for the ridge and hurried her way to the home of a woman who had recently lost her newborn son. She meant to leave the children here with this quiet family but she feared that she would be found out so once the children had been nursed, Marva began a trek that would eventually lead her to Crerar where she would find herself too exhausted to go on. She had travelled for over two months, walking most of the way. She accepted rides and help when she was in need but ultimately the children were her responsibility. Marva had to be realistic; she couldn't continue travelling with these infants ceaselessly. Nearing exhaustion, she spied a farm with her sorry eyes. The garden looked well tended and the woman who scrubbed clothing in a basin on the porch looked wholesome. Marva made a decision; she would leave the babies here on this farm. So it came to be that the Royal twins of Adnil grew up in Crerar with parents who would one day abandon them for the very reason that they almost lost their lives before they had lived out their first day.

Marva disappeared and lived out her life in fine style compared to her previous existence in Manek. The gold sovereign was enough to keep her well fed and happy for what remained of her life. It wasn't till she was close to death that she confided her story to a friend who was a magic user. This woman went on to join The Enclave when V's crawling web spell enticed her to go north. She was the harbinger of information that would be of great interest to her new master.

CHAPTER 20

EACH FLEETING MOMENT that Den had spent at the farm was time lost that could have been used in his search for Fannie. He rode Dash to her limits and arrived in the city as evening fell. Once he passed through the Southman Gates, the exhausted horse did not have the strength to carry him for the additional three hours it would take to reach the palace. He found a stable that would care for her needs and allow her the rest she needed after carrying Den on his harrowing ride. Den patted her on the neck and promised to see her very soon. He dug into his saddlebag and retrieved the scrap of parchment he and Jok had been given by The Society. He was not stopping to rest himself except to drink a pint of brew and gobble a gravy filled trencher. Den set out for the market area and found an idle cart runner. The muscled runner perked up when he laid eyes on Den's crumpled parchment. This was his ticket into the palace where the refreshments were plentiful and comforts were offered to those who had provided a service. A few hours of running would be well rewarded.

Den was too tired to enjoy the sights of the great city. Instead he took this opportunity to doze and relax his sore muscles. Before he knew it, the cart runner was slowing and a novice candidate was waving them toward the entryway of the welcoming building. Den jumped off the cart and requested an immediate audience with the chancellor. The candidate saw that Den was very agitated so she spent only moments directing the spent cart runner to the area where he could collect his payment, take part in refreshments and rest. She asked Den to follow her and they proceeded through the huge welcoming hall and made their way into the courtyard. Archel was sitting by a fountain with several other candidates and once she spied him, she excused herself and rushed in Den's direction. She dismissed the novice and thanked her for showing Den to the courtyard. He repeated his insistence to meet with the Chancellor and Archel assured him that they could be immediately on their way to his quarters. She was infected with Den's agitation so they both hurried to find the Chancellor in his private quarters. Archel knocked on a set of massive wooden doors that stood at the end of a beautifully decorated hallway. Den had no patience or interest in the décor and was tapping his foot impatiently when the doors slowly came apart. A maid showed them through the opulent chambers that were the Chancellor's home. Morgan was sitting in a chaise, by the fountain, in his private courtyard eating sweet confections. He initially registered surprise and delight to see Den back so soon but he quickly read the mood of the young man and his demeanour became one of concern.

Archel was allowed to stay with the two men as Den recounted the events of the last several days, beginning with his return to the farm. He described the carnage that he and Jok had encountered upon their return and he explained how El and the children had been hurt and mistreated. Morgan promised to dispatch a gifted member of The Society to the farm, where he would be able to heal Frederer and ease Nina's troubled young mind. Jok's family would receive the help they needed to get their lives back in order. Den was relieved because he had been racked with guilt over leaving Jok and El to deal with the children and the farm on their own.

Finding Fannie was another matter altogether; Morgan was afraid to encourage Den's optimism. The best he could do at this moment was to sympathize, console and promise to do whatever he could to help find the worried young man's sister. Fannie could be anywhere; she was a proverbial needle in a haystack. Morgan knew that what Den needed to do was hone his powers and discover how much strength he possessed before he could hope to be prepared to find Fannie. He needed Den assigned to a member who would guide him and teach him to discover his capabilities.

Morgan did his very best to calm Den and to show him the reason behind the only plausible plan to find Fannie. He systematically discussed the possibilities: Fannie could be dead or she could be hurt but these options were not probable. Someone had put forth a lot of effort to take Fannie captive, it was doubtful that anyone would have made off with her just to hurt or kill her. If they had meant to harm her, they could have accomplished that end right on the farm. Since Den knew, from Mica, that Fannie had been loaded into a wagon, reason led to the assumption that she was a valuable commodity to somebody.

The discussion with Morgan had calmed Den and he was ready to listen attentively to a reasonable plan to help his sister. The chancellor went on to convince Den to let The Society help him to control his powers so that when he needed to use his gifts, he would be prepared. This would take some time but Morgan promised to accelerate Den's program so that he could be ready, as soon as possible, to begin his search for Fannie. Morgan's logic was undeniable so Den agreed to stay and learn what he could. Archel suggested that Carl might be a good companion for Den because they were of the same age. Although Carl had been acting strangely over the past several weeks, Morgan agreed that he may serve as a liaison to Den.

CHAPTER 21

A LAY PERSON HAD been dispatched to retrieve Dash from the stable where Den had left her. Den exercised her every morning, riding her bareback on the beach, along the area of hard packed sand where the surf washed back and forth over her hooves. She seemed to enjoy the feeling of freedom that the beach provided and she missed her master if he ever missed a day. Carl did most things with Den but he was unprepared to ride a horse. He explained that he was more of a wagon kind of person. They spent most of their free time together and they also attended the same group lessons which focused on Society protocols. Den spent each afternoon with his personal tutor who was helping him to actually use his gifts. Den remembered how he and Fannie had used their powers to accomplish a variety of things in the past but using his own powers, without her, felt very different. It felt as though some ingredient was missing from his recipe for power.

Quay'Sea was appointed as Den's private tutor and he was also the most senior member of The Society. Besides Morgan, no one had been with The Society longer than this faithful man. Morgan needed his best friend's help with this complex situation. He could trust this man with his own life so he could certainly rely on him to understand the importance of accelerating Den's training. Morgan also planned to confide in Quay'Sea with a secret that would put his life in jeopardy. Morgan would tell him who Den really was.

It was by a lucky coincidence that Morgan had run into an old woman who was shopping for produce at Morgan's favourite vendor's shop. The apples and peaches were undeniably the ripest and juiciest fruit to be had in all of Manek. Mango had a reputation for quality fruit in each of his several locations, found in every quadrant of Manek. The old woman recognised Morgan as an old friend of the late King. She approached him shyly and whispered that she had some information that he would find very interesting. Always a fan of intrigue and a fine meal, Morgan invited the woman to dine with him at a quaint little establishment not far from Mango's.

They occupied a table in the rear of the pub where Morgan ordered more food than the two could possibly eat in 3 days. He had been kept in suspense long enough; he ate while the woman talked. In the next few moments, Morgan lost all interest in the feast and sat dumbfounded as the woman spun her tale. She had been the midwife who had attended the late Queen D'Enfanel on the day that the "would be" prince had been stillborn. Now, years later, the woman felt there was no harm in telling Morgan the truth of what actually occurred on that fateful day. The King and Queen were both dead and the country was in the hands of the beloved royal couple, Zelebeth and Archer. She had kept her secret long enough. She never knew for sure if she actually did it, but she had given her mute and almost blind assistant Marva the grizzly task of disposing of the twins. The Queen had borne healthy twins but chose to present the King with a stillborn boy child acquired in the poor section of Manek. It was their eyes; the woman explained to Morgan, each of the infants had one emerald and one violet eye. This was a sure sign of Magic and everyone knew how the Queen felt about gifted people. She wanted her own children drowned and forgotten, as though they had never existed. In her heart, the woman believed that Marva had made off with the babes because she had never been heard from again. The Queen had paid her well to keep this secret and she hoped that Morgan would now pay her for having told him the truth. Morgan did pay for the information and he continued to pay the woman, to this very day, to keep her secret between only Morgan and herself.

Since he had learned about the possibility that these twins had survived, Morgan had been using Society resources to search for them. Carlotta was the investigator who finally found the pair, hidden right under their noses, a hard day's ride from Manek.

Fannie had been stolen from her home and Den would have been taken as well if he hadn't been here, at The Society's stronghold, with his farmer companion, Jok. Morgan was keenly aware that he had not been the only one searching for Den and Fannie. Someone else obviously knew about them and wanted them just as badly as Morgan did. He had to trust someone else with all this information to ensure that it could be passed on if some accident should befall him. His mind was made up, Quay'Sea was his most trusted friend and he was also suited to be the perfect tutor for Den.

CHAPTER 22

DEN'S EDUCATION MOVED along swiftly. Under the skilled tutelage of Quay'Sea, Den was discovering his newly nurtured abilities daily. He was initially tested to see what he could affect. Den's gifts gave him influence over the dominions of fire, water, air and earth. He was described as multi-gifted by Quay'Sea who had never encountered a candidate with so much versatility. Den's lessons included learning to call upon all of these elements and to have them do his bidding.

He was made to read scrolls, tablets and bindings where he gained the knowledge of symbols and signatures which could be used to increase his power. He practiced drawing these magical codes using several media. He worked with sand, salt, metals, gems and a variety of liquids. Memorizing the designs was a necessity since he would never be able to carry scrolls and tablets with him. He was constantly tested and questioned to ensure that he was absorbing and maintaining what he had learned. Den proved to be quite an accomplished protégé and never failed to impress his teacher.

They began with water. Every afternoon and sometimes late into the evening, he worked with his tutor to cause water to appear, disappear, flow and be held at bay. He was giddy the day that he walked into the ocean and caused the water to open a pathway for him so that he could walk along the sandy bottom with walls of water bordering his path. For Den, this seemed like a silly trick; he was enchanted to watch the fish swim right up to the edge of his barrier, but Quay'Sea was stunned that his novice wielded such advanced command. Morgan received reports each evening detailing Den's achievements and Quay'Sea met with his chancellor to plan new trials for the young man.

Den's skills were just as impressive when he worked with air, fire and earth. There was little he could not accomplish with direction. Soon enough, Den was creating his own trials and succeeding in most of his attempts.

One day, as he was riding Dash along the shore when her hoof suddenly snagged on a piece of well anchored seaweed and caused her to lose her footing. As she was falling Den drew his powers instantly and caused her to be lifted into the air and fly, with him still on her back, along the beach. He managed to calm the terrified horse so that she could land safely. Quay'Sea understood that Den could now use his powers creatively when the circumstance demanded inventiveness. There would always be more for Den to learn but in only one season, he had procured more than enough skill to begin his quest for Fannie. Den was anxious to begin his quest and The Society wanted Fannie back almost as much as Den did.

Everything that Den had learned had been laced with the virtues that The Society insisted upon. Compassion, honesty, love, concern, help, health, kindness: these were all valid reasons to use one's gifts. Magic was sacred and the gifts themselves were treasures which must be treated with reverence and always used with righteous intentions. The dark arts were forbidden even though their magic was ultimately the same. Magic was either black or white depending on the intention with which it was used. Doing harm was absolutely taboo. Once a Sorcerer was tempted with dark purpose, it was difficult to move back toward a virtuous intent. Greed and the need to control others for personal gain had turned several gifted individuals toward choosing the dark arts and they had faced various consequences for their actions.

Den was an innately good person so The Society was not concerned that he would be tempted to move toward the dark arts. If this had been a possibility, Morgan would have halted his education at once. Den had opened his mind to both Morgan and Quay'Sea during his edification, in an effort to commune with his mentors more straightforwardly. What they saw in Den's mind was reassuring; he held fast to all the virtues that they held dear. The only secret they kept from Den was that of his origin. It was not yet the time to burden him with that information and what it would mean for the future for both him and Fannie.

Den never expected anyone to behave in a way that was unethical. He believed that everyone had a core that was good and loving. This faith would become the reason why he would eventually be disillusioned and betrayed by a companion whom he valued and trusted.

Carl was staggered by his good fortune when he had been assigned to act as Den's liaison. He had squirreled himself close to his new friend and promptly became Den's confidante. Carl was always available when Den had a bad day or an exceptional day. He helped him to celebrate his accomplishments and consoled him when things did not work out as planned. Their rooms were side by side and they often sat and talked late into the night. Den had no reason to believe that Carl had anything but good intentions. One evening, when Den was missing Fannie, he confided in Carl. He told him that he was eager to begin searching for her. He understood why he needed to hone his skills but every day without Fannie was torture. Carl counselled Den to rush his mentors as much as possible and he vowed to personally accompany Den when he left on his quest. Den appreciated his friend's compassion and took Carl at his word that they would search for Fannie together. Duplicity was not within Den's understanding so he accepted Carl as his best friend.

Carl was keeping V well informed with all things concerning Den. A number of pigeons had made their way north carrying information documenting Den's abilities and his personal thoughts. V was encouraged and pleased that Carl schemed to accompany Den on his search for Fannie. Den would have no surprises for V. He would be expected in the north when he was finally led there.

CHAPTER 23

FANNIE WAS ADJUSTING to her captivity mainly because she was treated as a visitor and not a prisoner. Her new friends, Shilinar and Mushookoalah, whom she affectionately dubbed Shilly and Mushy, were her constant companions. She inherently trusted the odd couple and they had both grown very fond of her. The boys didn't know it at the time but their friendship with Fannie was the only reason that they were still healthy guests at the Enclave.

V's web-crawler spell brought numerous magicians to the north but many of them were not useful candidates for the wielding of the dark arts. Those individuals who did not possess even a small shred of evil and were abhorred by witnessing suffering were not apt to ever be candidates who could be expected to inflict misery or affliction. Some people were just innately good. They could not be coaxed by greed so they found themselves no longer welcomed. Because compassion was not one of V's merits, he most often just muddled their minds and sent these unfortunates out into the cold to fend for themselves. They wandered the arctic wasteland, without food or water, until their bodies succumbed to the elements and they just died. Such was the fate that awaited Shilly and Mushy until Fannie chose them as her compatriots. V justified all this wasteful death by rationalizing that, at the very least, he was ensuring that these white magicians would never live to join The Society. They would never get the opportunity to work against him. V intended to begin Fannie's education very soon so he did not want her upset by the disappearance of her newly forged friends, so they lived, so long as Fannie lived.

V maintained a firm hope that Fannie possessed at least a small fibre of evil in her being so that she would not be forced to endure the fate of all those candidates who were barred from the castle and obliged to face the elements. His faith in his ability to educate Fannie to use the dark arts was purely selfish; he wanted her on his side, but if V couldn't turn her, he would kill her. She could not be allowed to live and pose a possible threat to V's planned domination. He needed to find a kernel within Fannie that he could work with, like he had with so many candidates before her. Carl was turning out to be quite a success for V. With fortune on his side, V was certain that he would succeed with Fannie as well.

V couldn't let Fannie begin to explore her gifs until he was sure that he could mould her in the image he desired. She had to trust him enough to let him into her mind so that he could search for the crack where he could place his wedge. He sincerely wished for that crack to exist or all of his plans would have been for naught. In their innocence, the two boys who had attached themselves to Fannie might be of some use. If Fannie opened her mind to either of them, V could strip her thoughts from their weaker and wide open minds. He had already been in their heads and they were not gifted enough to put up any obstructions much less barriers that could keep him out. Patience was the one and only virtue that could be attributed to V. He was willing to wait. V mused that an opportunity always presented itself to one who lingered and stayed alert. He made himself laugh out loud at the thought of waiting and staying alert because that was just the fate he had arranged for poor Manfred and dear Lily. They were destined to be patient as they watched and listened for an opportunity that would never come to them. People had to remember not to anger him. He really did have a very bad temper.

Fannie, Shilly and Mushy idled their time away exploring the castle and amusing themselves playing mind enhancing games. There were number games and all sorts of gambling which motivated the players to learn how to play the odds. Oversized chess sets, made of the same rock as the rest of the dreary Enclave, sat on many of the tables in the common rooms. Mushy was a master of that game and spent hours teaching Shilly and Fannie the rules and the strategies required to win. They played against each other while Mushy usually chose a formidable opponent who could challenge his skill. Molisana, a slim and plain looking young girl from a small village in the foothills of the Borealis Mountains, challenged anyone to defeat her. She was the current chess champion and was very pompous about her title. Molisana coveted the title and had defended her trophy many times. The three were alone in the huge room and Shilly and Fannie decided to play a friendly game while Mushy gave advice and instruction when Molisana strutted into the common, followed by her entourage. Her arrogance was apparent when she sneered at Mushy and told Fannie that if she wanted to master the game of chess, she should find an able teacher. Mushy was not the type of person who would ever take offence over a hurtful remark but he was quite a proficient chess master. Rather than let Molisana go on her way with her admiring cluster of followers, his pride took control and he smiled and challenged her to test his skills. Molisana could not walk away from a challenge, especially with her clique eagerly egging her on. A table was set and Mushy won the choosing; he would play the white pieces.

The game was played with the finesse that only two masters could display. They played neck and neck losing the same number of pieces so that no one player ever dominated the board. The onlookers were growing tense as the players went into the end game. Molisana didn't show it but she was very worried that this Mushy may well win the game and she could not allow that to happen.

She was a powerful candidate with dominion over minds, thoughts and emotions. She was almost advanced enough in her skills to become a member of the Enclave and this Mushy had yet to begin his education. Molisana sent her mind to Mushy in an attempt to touch his emotions and make him nervous and unsure. Mushy broke out in a cold sweat and did seem to become a little drained. He concentrated harder and was still in the game when Molisana had had enough and she sent Mushy a muddling spell which occupied a small crevasse of his mind and served to completely befuddle him. The game was lost and Molisana made a great deal of gloating over her own superiority and skill. She led her group out of the common, all the while degrading and insulting poor Mushy. Fannie and Shilly consoled their distressed friend and did their best to lift his spirits. Mushy didn't understand what had come over him; he had the game won when he had been abruptly overcome with self doubt and anxiety which still persisted. He was extremely nervous and unable to calm down. Fannie was so moved by Mushy's distress that she opened her mind and sent him consoling thoughts and feelings of happiness and joy. Mushy was still recovering his equilibrium when he suddenly shrugged off his loss, changed his mood and decided to not let it bother him further. Fannie had helped him to feel like himself again and she had done it without even a moment of hesitation. She hadn't shared anyone's mind since that awful day at the farm. Letting her mind free, even if just for a moment, had made her feel free and useful after all this time behind her personal barrier. A nice long walk exploring the castle would cheer them all up.

V surreptitiously scanned Shilly and Mushy on an ongoing basis. Their gifts were weak and neither of them could register someone in their minds.

V was waiting for one of them to make a connection with Fannie. She would have to be the one who initiated the contact because those two clods could never master the necessary skills of their own accord. V could barely tolerate being in their minds, their weakness sickened him. Today, V would be rewarded for all of his patience.

Late that evening, V rested in his cold chamber dressed in light cotton, when Moira carried in a tray filled with refreshments for herself and her master. V admired her provocative attire and wondered what this night had in store. They ate slowly while they chatted about the day's events and plotted about their plans for the near future. They were anticipating the arrival of Den and Carl; they needed to develop a scheme to keep the twins apart till Fannie's fate could be decided. If V determined that Fannie could be educated, Den would most probably be easier to turn. Thinking about Fannie reminded V to casually cast out his mind and search for the bumbling Shilinar and the chubby Mushookoalah. When he touched Mushy's mind he physically jumped as though he had been touched by lightening. Fannie had finally found a reason to open her mind; this was the event that V had been anticipating.

Mushy was napping after a healthy dinner that had warmed him enough to find temporary comfort from his frigid existence. He went from a dreamy sleep to total unconsciousness as V urgently slammed his mind into Mushy's and began to ravage random corners of his thoughts to gather any clue of Fannie that may have remained there. He slowed his search in an effort to systematically search every possible corner of this sluggish mind. V's painstaking search was measured and this was the only thing that saved Mushy from eventually waking as a complete idiot. If V's search had continued to be frantic, Mushy would have regained consciousness but he would never have maintained his ability to think; his mind would have been left permanently muddled. Moira stared at V as he sat in his chair focusing all of his concentration on his task. A satisfied smile spread across his face and Moira knew that Fannie had made the ultimate mistake; she had opened her mind. V came back into his own and shared his new information with his concubine.

He had found the shard that he had hoped would be there. No one else ever entered this lout's mind and V had been very cautious to leave no essence of himself inside Mushookoalah, so Fannie must have left this precious flotsam when she had consoled her ridiculous friend. Fannie was almost unfailingly good but this tidbit that she left in her friend's mind was the evidence that V needed to begin her education. Fannie possessed arrogance. V had found it where it had not existed in the past. Mushookoalah was proud and this was a vice but he had never been arrogant so V was sure that Fannie could be turned to accept and wield the dark arts.

CHAPTER 24

FANNIE'S SCHEDULE LEFT her with very little time to spend with Mushy and Shilly. They used to eat leisurely and spend hours either playing games, exploring or just sitting and talking. Mushy had taken ill the evening before Fannie was informed that her education was to begin. Shilly spent most of his time ministering his ailing companion but he was miserable without Fannie. Mushy was continually dizzy and experienced difficulty with his balance and his eyesight. Heavily bundled, he slept for hours at a time which left Shilly with a lot of time to read as he watched over his best friend. Shilly determined that Mushy just needed to get warm for a time; that might set him back to normal.

He borrowed one text at a time from the library that the group had discovered during one of their explorations. They had dubbed it "the lost library" because the labyrinth they had to solve each time they visited was always different. It was a long walk and he had to solve the changing labyrinth every time he wanted to access the library but he had little else to do while his friend lay sleeping. No one attended the library so Shilly assumed that the books were available to the candidates who showed an interest.

Shilly knew his powers were weak but he did have a skill that no one had recognised or tapped. He possessed a photographic memory and back in Kingsport, he had been able to recite the epic songs presented by the travelling bards after he had heard them only once. When he saw pictures or puzzles, he could recreate them precisely, right down to the finest detail. He was an artist. Best of all, he knew how to read and understand almost any language after either hearing it or seeing it in its written form for only a few moments. This skill made reading the books from the lost library less complicated since each of the texts was written in a differing form of several unusual languages. Shilly read about spells and wards. He learned about symbols and signatures and what they represented. He learned all the words of power that were carefully inscribed in texts that appeared ancient. The use of gems and fine metals to produce intricate charms and jewellery was of particular interest to Shilly because of his artistic background. Memorizing as he read, Shilly was becoming a human guide to the use of magic. He pondered what he could actually achieve with all this knowledge if he only had more power. He did not crave the power; this is what made Shilly very different from V.

Fannie stopped in to visit with the boys whenever she was allowed a free moment. Mushy was always asleep and Shilly was reading. He told her how much he missed having her company and Fannie knew exactly how he felt. It seemed that once one started one's education at the Enclave there was a consistent urgency to achieve. Fannie was exhausted every night by the time she finally drank some hot chai and bundled herself up to sleep for the three hours she was allotted. She couldn't remember any of the other candidates having followed such a gruelling timetable but maybe she had been too indifferent to have taken any notice. By the time Mushy was well enough to be up and around, Fannie had been diagnosed by her personal tutor. Although V would have preferred to mentor Fannie himself, he chose to err on the side of caution. He wanted to distance himself so that Fannie would not recognise his pressing interest in her progress. V appointed one of his most talented minions to introduce Fannie to her own gifts.

Bardook was Fannie's age and he looked as though he could have been related to her. His complexion was very fair and his hair was black and curled in a dazzling cascade. He usually wore his unruly locks tied at the nape of his neck with an artfully crafted pendant much like Jeeree's. He was a senior member at the Enclave even though he appeared far too young to have achieved this station. Only V knew that Bardook was actually over 100 years old; his powers allowed him to arrest his own aging. His dominant dominion was the controlling of time and its passage. He also specialized in the crafting of signatures and symbols much like Moira did. He had considerable magical strength but his advantage lay in his ability to amplify his power with the use of symbols like the ones he'd crafted into his hair pendant.

Bardook and Fannie shared almost every waking moment together. His first priority was to determine what magical territories this wisp of a girl had the potential to control. With Fannie's mind barriers soundly anchored in place, Bardook was left with little more than verbal instruction to educate this stubborn girl. If she would only project into his mind she could learn the techniques and carry out his instructions with greater competence. V had forbidden Bardook to coerce Fannie in any way that would make her uncomfortable or suspicious of his intentions. V was the master and his commands were not to be questioned so Bardook was justified when reporting that Fannie's progress was painstakingly slow. It took time and patience for Bardook to explain, demonstrate and re-explain simple modus operandi for Fannie to employ.

Bardook was trying to enlighten Fannie about the ways in which she could send out her thoughts to an individual while continuing to barricade her own mind from any reverse probes. This was a lesson that was of profound interest to Fannie. She laboured for days, sending Bardook tiny tendrils of thought, trying to read his mind without letting him glide back into her psyche along that same fragile thread. Each time Bardook seemed to be moving toward her mind, Fannie snapped the link and kept her privacy intact. While in his mind, Fannie gathered much information and was able to cooperate with his instructions to a higher degree of effectiveness. She was also intrigued by Bardook's secrets; he kept many puzzling areas of his mind dark and unapproachable. Fannie had never encountered an individual with a mind so crowded with recesses, avenues and mazes. It appeared as though Bardook had stored the thoughts of several lifetimes inside himself.

The tasks that Bardook set for Fannie were easier for her to complete with the free access into his mind that she had now mastered. His instructions were vivid and clear and his virtual demonstrations were succinct when she read them directly from his thoughts. So far, Fannie's dominions spanned a wide gamut and included gifts directed toward the influence of health and well-being, basic physicality, mind control as well as climate and weather manipulation. Bardook encouraged Fannie to steel her will and direct her focus on the tasks she attempted to complete. She put forth all of her efforts to glean as much information as she could because she did have a hidden agenda. She needed the means to escape this prison castle and she needed enough power and knowledge to take her two friends with her.

Bardook had witnessed Fannie turn a clear sky grey and cause snow to fall. She had succeeded in causing a broken leg to heal when a novice had arrived at the Enclave after a sledding accident. Fannie could cause objects to disappear and reappear in a different location. She continued to be able to maintain her mind barrier even under assault. Bardook had warned her that he would randomly try to enter her mind so he could test her protective abilities. Even while she slept, her mind remained her personal fortress; she could now venture into the minds of almost any other candidates and even most members.

Fannie displayed the diverse characteristics usually seen in either magic users, sorceresses or even witches, but very rarely observed at the same time in the same individual. She was certainly a prize and Bardook was gaining respect for Fannie's abilities and beginning to comprehend V's immense interest in this raven haired young conjurer. Bardook consulted with V and, with trepidation, recommended that Fannie begin to be allowed to read the books which would teach her the arts of wards and signatures. V had no misgivings and encouraged Bardook to give Fannie access to the Enclave libraries. Even V could not have foreseen the power that was building inside of Fannie; she had not yet encountered a reason to unleash her capabilities but that day was fast approaching.

CHAPTER 25

LIFE IN THE opulent surroundings of The Society's locale was becoming very comfortable for Den. Now, that he felt secure with his abilities to wield his gifts with adequate power, he started to feel the anxiety caused by the fleeting of time. Somewhere out there, his sister was alone and in the clutches of her unknown assailants. Morgan was stalling Den and providing weak excuses in an attempt to delay Den's departure. Den complained bitterly to his most trusted comrade, Carl, who appeared supportive while actually orchestrating his own clandestine plans for their unscheduled departure.

Morgan was suspicious of Carl's recent behaviours. The boy spent too much time in the rookery with those messy pigeons. He ordered a surreptitious surveillance of Carl so it could be determined who he had been keeping contact with. Morgan wanted to be sure of Carl's veracity before he assigned him to the detail that would soon travel with Den. A talented candidate named Apel, who was skilled with all manner of living beasts, was waiting patiently above the rise for a pigeon to be let loose from its tower. He would coax it down and read the message it carried. Carl had been in the rookery for over and hour so Apel expected to be back in the mess in time to eat while the food was still hot. Only a few brief moments passed before Carl leaned over the side of the tower and released his message carrier. As soon as Carl was no longer in sight, Apel exerted his will upon the bird and it flew directly toward him and landed on his shoulder. He read and memorized the cryptic message, hoping that it would hold some meaning to Morgan. Written in a slanted script, the message simply read:

The time for departure is at hand.
Shroud our way.
C

The bird was sent on its way so that its intended receiver would not be made suspicious by a missing message that may be expected. Apel made his way to the office of the chancellor to report his findings but found that Morgan was nowhere to be found. Rather than wait, he decided to join the other candidates in the mess for the evening meal. After dinner a number of the novices and the several older candidates were planning a gathering on the beach where they planned to build a large fire and cavort the evening away. Apel was never one to miss out on an entertaining evening which promised the possibility of stealing a kiss from a willing young girl. So it came to pass that Morgan did not receive news of the obscure message until well into the following day. By that time it was too late to change the course of events that had transpired.

Carl used all of his influence to convince an eager Den that they needed to sneak away and initiate the search for Fannie. If they waited until Morgan finally decided to allow them his permission, Fannie could be lost. He worked Den's emotions into a frenzy until he had him totally convinced that Morgan had some furtive reason to keep him from his quest. Carl promised that he could make it possible for them to leave The Society's enclosure without raising an alarm or even being observed. Den paid close attention as Carl disclosed his plan. They would leave tonight and no one would be aware of their departure until late the following morning.

Carl was not looking forward to riding a horse but he had been unable to plan an escape that did not include needing fast transportation. As soon as they had finished eating, Den and Carl made their way to the stables. Den saddled Dash and helped his friend to choose and saddle a black stallion, named Brock that appeared to have taken to Carl. With saddle bags packed and loaded, they rode out behind the stabling area and made for the beach which was Dash's favourite place to run. She took the lead and Brock enjoyed the unexpected freedom as he ran along behind her. They headed north and kept to the beach until they neared the Northman shipyards. Here they found a gentle embankment where the horses could climb up to the meet the crowded streets of the Northman region of Manek. The dock side areas were filled with unsavoury groups of individuals who were best avoided. Carl led the way because he was familiar with this locale and Den stayed close behind him as the sun set in the west.

They had made their way through Manek by midnight and were passing through the last Northman gate under a sky filled with stars. Den admired the twinkling lightshow and wondered if Fannie was somewhere looking at the same sky and thinking of him. Carl suggested that they travel through the night so that they could put as much distance as possible between themselves and Manek before morning. Carl kept them moving northward along the coast at a slow and steady pace to ensure that the horses did not become injured. As dawn broke, Carl and Den were crossing the Adnak/Kandar border. They stopped to rest and water the horses at a creek that emptied into the sea. The two men were weary and unsteady on their feet after their gruelling night ride. Den insisted that they sleep for a time before they decided where they would go from here. This suited Carl just fine because he needed the time to send an overpowering suggestion into Den's mind. His ultimate plan was coming to fruition in a fashion more precisely than he could have hoped for.

Den unrolled his blanket and found a soft place in the grass close to where he had tethered the horses. They could graze and rest while Den slept close by. Carl was washing his face and neck in the creek and Den assumed that he would get some sleep once he had taken care of his comforts. Den's dreams were filled with images of Fannie. She was cold and ice surrounded her; her face was sad and her eyes pleaded for rescue.

Carl sat cross-legged beside his slumbering companion and hovered his hands, palms down, over Den's head. He gathered his will and deeply concentrated on the idea he planned to plant into Den's mind. Go north. Short and simple suggestions were the most successful and Carl wanted Den to choose the direction for their search. He would be content to follow as Den led him closer and closer to his master. With the suggestion firmly in place, Carl curled up to get some sleep before Den woke and resolved to pursue a northerly course.

By noon the men had eaten their rations and were on their way north at Den's stubborn insistence. They stayed with the coast and eventually stopped near a wooded area where they built a small fire and brewed some chai and ate some hard cheese and flatbread. Carl produced some maps that he had tucked in his saddle bag. He spread the maps on the grass and studied their possible routes. Den wanted to keep moving north; maybe Fannie was sending him some kind of message to lead him in her direction.

Carl explained their options; they could ride west as the coast turned, toward Port Merle or they could ride directly north through Kandar toward The Bay of Glaciers. There would be boats and barges at Port Merle that ploughed their way north along the Madyar coast. These were sailed by the fishers who hunted the sea monsters in the far north. They came south to trade their catch for the goods and services available in Port Merle. If they chose to ride north, to The Bay of Glaciers, the horses would quickly become useless in the deep snow and the treacherous ice. They would be fortunate to arrive at The Bay of Glaciers with two healthy horses. After giving the matter some thought, Den decided to cast his luck with finding a barge to take them north. The horses could be boarded at Port Merle, where they could be retrieved on the way back.

Carl was secretly pleased with Den's choice; he was not an enthusiast of the dogsled ride, through Afshen, that could take between 12 and 20 days depending on the weather conditions. He had been on one of those sleds in the past and he did not plan to choose this mode of transportation when there was an alternative. Carl loved his master but he did not enjoy the cold as V did. He had been delighted with his assignment at Manek with The Society. He did not accept their moral indignation but, he had to admit, they knew how to be comfortable and their location boasted the most temperate climate in the entire world. He missed the gentle sea breeze already; soon he'd be facing the blistering winds of his master's domain. He wondered what had possessed V to choose such a remote and inclement location for his Enclave.

Four days riding along the Bay coast brought the men into the Port of Merle. It was not to be compared to Manek, but it was a busy and colourful place. The roads were wide and the people were friendly. Den and Carl found an inn located close to the main docks where all the ships loaded and unloaded their bounties. The stables were acceptable and a small boy who tended the horses was happy to exercise Dash and Brock for a meagre copper.

From the inn, the men could watch for a ship that would be willing to take them north. Carl knew that V would have sent out a spell that would be confusing anyone who may be following them but he still wished that passage on a ship would make itself available soon.

CHAPTER 26

APEL RUBBED HIS pounding head as he walked across the common. Too much mead on the beach; he would suffer till late afternoon paying for his imbibing habit. He craved the hot tea that would soothe his dry throat and rejuvenate his rasping voice before he made his way to sit and wait for his turn to see the chancellor. He would have to learn to live with disappointment where his tea was concerned. The chancellor was rushing toward him from behind the fountain. Den and Carl were missing and no one seemed to know where they could be. A search was underway to see if they could be somewhere on the grounds. Morgan wanted to know if Apel had any information as to their whereabouts. Apel related the only information he had; he had last seen Carl exiting the tower after he had sent his pigeon on its way. That had been just before evening meal the previous day. Morgan was beside himself with irritation and impatience. Apel admitted that he had intercepted the pigeon and he used his mind to project a visual image of the cryptic message to Morgan. Morgan saw it just the way it had appeared to Apel yesterday afternoon.

The time for departure is at hand.
Shroud our way.
C

This was turning into a debacle for Morgan. At this moment a runner arrived to report that Den's horse was missing along with a black stallion. Morgan knew that the missing young men would not be found on The Society's grounds. They were gone and Den didn't know that he was accompanied by a spy. The chancellor had to keep a clear head; the first thing he had to do was devise a plan to follow Den and Carl, wherever they may have gone. He sent a runner to summon Quay'Sea to meet him in his office and rushed off in that direction.

Morgan and Quay'Sea sat in the main office, silently contemplating their next possible actions. They agreed to shuffle through the gifts available to them in any and all of the members and candidates at The Society. They required someone with the ability to follow the trail of a shrouding spell. They also needed someone who could search for Den's mind over long distances. Groups of investigators should be sent to random locations where they could inquire about two men travelling on horseback. They could describe the men and the horses and blind luck may provide some clue to the direction the pair had taken. Morgan was satisfied that they had considered all the possibilities and he began giving orders, mobilizing all the people who needed to be involved in the search. The homing pigeons were crated and distributed to every search party. All information was to be sent back to The Society as soon as it was discovered. Alone, Morgan would coordinate from here because Quay'Sea insisted on leaving with a team, for he believed that he had the best chance of contacting Den's mind.

Carlotta led the group comprised of Quay'Sea and two candidates who were gifted with the ability to identify a spell in action. They anticipated finding the shroud mentioned in the message Carl had sent. Just before they left the grounds, Apel had suddenly recalled that the pigeon had flown north when he re-released it. He caught up with Carlotta and this information caused her to turn her group toward the north. They were a full day's ride behind the young men and Carlotta was already suffering the symptoms of her proximity to her horse. Quay'Sea was able to help by encasing Carlotta in a bubble of fresh air where the stench of the horse did not penetrate. She was relieved and able to ride more comfortably. Where had this magician been all those years that Carlotta had walked the countryside because of her affliction?

Because the young men had travelled through the night and only stopped to sleep for a short time, the search party was actually further behind than they imagined. The thoughts that Quay'Sea cast out in random directions to try to connect with Den were incapable of contacting him over such a vast distance. The candidates, named Bin and Churl, were experiencing disorientation when they searched for the shroud. They determined that this spell must have been cast by a powerful sorcerer to have such an effect on both of them.

At the end of their second day heading north, they came to the crossroads where they would have to decide whether to turn west toward Port of Merle or continue toward The Bay of Glaciers. They considered splitting up but they needed all of their combined skills to make the search plausible. Carlotta tossed a coin and left their fate to chance since no one had a clever reason to choose either direction. They would head for The Bay of Glaciers together. It would be at least 6 days travel and some of that would most probably be on foot because the horses would not be able to carry their additional weight over the snowy and icy terrain.

CHAPTER 27

DEN AND CARL walked down to the dock to meet a barge that had just begun unloading huge blocks of frozen meat. This was what they had been waiting for; a way north. The fishers were happy to accept 20 coppers and the promise of hard work from these city dwellers who thought they wanted to voyage to Ice Port. Did these boys have the slightest clue what it was like up there? One of the fishers warned them to pack some winter wear unless they planned to look a lot like the frozen meat that was being carted off to be cooked, salted or dried at the fish market. Carl was well aware of the conditions he would be facing but he was unable to tell Den too much lest he arouse undue suspicion. Carl also knew that their destination was not Ice Port but North Point, the sight of the Enclave. These fishers would be familiar with the castle located on the point where they rounded and turned their vessel south. Carl would wait and see if Den decided to be put on shore at the salt covered castle.

Within a week, the barge was making its way north with two travellers who worked for their passage. When the Western Sea gave way to the Northern Sea, Den pulled on the fur lined overcoat and gloves that he had bartered for at the market in Port of Merle. The hood was snug and kept the winds from freezing his tender ears. As the barge pushed its way between ice bergs Den donned the leg coverings and fur lined boots to keep his feet and legs from frostbite that the fishers had warned against. Carl had purchased similar garb because he already knew what conditions he would face on this floating nightmare.

They watched the coastline of Madyar as they moved sluggishly north. Den saw huge beasts emerge from the sea to cavort on the beach as though they were small puppies rolling around in the grass. He and Carl were leaning on the rail when the shadow of the castle came into view. It was colossal. Den was stunned by its grandeur even though it stood like a lonely sentinel decorated in shades of grey and white. From this distance, he could just make out the silhouette of a woman, standing out against the bright sky, on the highest tower of the bastion. He automatically sent out a thread of thought to search for Fannie, just as he had every day along their journey. As of yet, he had never received a reply but he never encountered what he felt right now either. Rather than the nothing he was expecting, he registered a barrier that he couldn't penetrate. He also sensed many minds that would welcome his thought but he pulled back before his probe was revealed to anyone. Den dragged Carl along to find the captain of the vessel. He needed to get off this barge here, at this frozen castle. The captain was hesitant to drop his charges in this remote location near the castle that was avoided by anyone who was sane. They never even paused to fish this area because too many strange and unexplained occurrences had manifested themselves in and around these waters. They had seen people waving from the shore but there was no place to get close enough to hear what they shouted. How could he drop them here with no way to escape the elements if they were not welcomed at the castle? Den was frantic and he finally offered the captain a silver coin for a small craft that he and Carl could row to shore. The captain was not these men's keeper. If they wanted to risk their very lives on this fool's quest and pay him a full silver for a boat barely worth 10 coppers, who was he to refuse? As the barge slowed for its turn to the east, toward Ice Port, the deck hands lowered Carl and Den in a dinghy, equipped with two oars and nothing else, into the punishing Northern Sea.

As the barge slowly disappeared on the horizon, Den and Carl rowed with all their strength toward an uninviting, rocky coast. This small wooden boat would not survive the beating it would take when it was smashed against the cruel shore. Den lifted his oar, gathered his power and concentrated. Carl watched as Den calmed the waters around the boat and stilled the punishing winds that were blowing them back out to sea. They rowed easily to the shore and stowed the boat against a large granite boulder that hid it from the castle.

Carl could plant suggestions into people's minds but he could not send his thoughts at will like Den could. If he had had that power, V would already know that Den was delivered. As it happened, Fannie would be the first to know that Den was here. Carl knew a secret entry way into the castle and guided Den in the general direction without making it appear that he knew where he was heading. A doorway built into the side of the solid rock structure led to a long hallway ending in a staircase that led downwards. The stairs were also hewn from solid rock. One of Den's dominions was earth and he was curious so he probed the rock. This rock was moulded by magic. Den expanded his probe and sensed that the entire structure had been created using powerful magic. Carl was looking nervous and Den planned to send his friend some calming thoughts. When he entered Carls mind, everything was explained in one agonizing moment. His friend was really his enemy. He was leading him here to be imprisoned just as his sister was. Den felt a fury building in him. Fuelled by the dejection he felt and the overwhelming betrayal of his would be comrade, Den hurled his emotions toward Carl; the air gathered around his outstretched arm and shot forward to knock Carl against the solid rock wall. He hung there, unconscious, held in place by Den's will. Den couldn't have Carl raising an alarm so he concentrated on the ice which littered the floor, until it melted over Carl and refroze, pinning him in place. Carl had no powers that could release him from this frozen confinement. If someone found him soon enough he would live, otherwise the elements would take him. Den felt no compassion for this man who was a friend to those that came to Jok's farm and caused so much damage and hurt.

Den was drained, not from using his powers but rather from the heart-rending emotions which seemed to weaken him and suck any remaining strength out of him. He felt as though he could just sit down and cry, like he was a little boy again, with a scraped knee. He did actually sit down but when he caught sight of Carl, partially frozen to the rock wall, the vision fuelled his resolve to finish this quest. He knew he was close to Fannie but he was trapped under the lair of the one who had kidnapped her. That individual was obviously very powerful to have created this fortress so Den needed to exercise caution.

CHAPTER 28

CARLOTTA WAS SPENT by the effort it required to walk on her new nemesis that everyone called "snow". Sending her here had been fate's insidious plan to torture her further by keeping her away from the place she loved best—The Society grounds. She was just venting within her own mind, considering the injustice of having luck choose the northern fork at the crossroads. She could have been at The Port of Merle where the necessities and comforts of life were readily available. Her respect for all things supernatural caused Carlotta to pause and to thank her lucky star that her group had been able to barter for outerwear at a small village that they had passed through. Without these fur lined coats and leg coverings, they may well have succumbed to the harsh temperatures by now.

The wind had intensified its force and the sky promised more precipitation . . . more snow. Quay'Sea scanned the horizon of tree tops and was certain that he had seen some smoke rising. He navigated the group toward that general vicinity and soon they could all smell a fire burning. Their path intersected a road that was little used but easier to walk along than the forest trail they had been following since they had lost the road in a snowstorm. The tree-scape opened to reveal several small huts, haphazardly clustered around a large central building that appeared to be a trading post. It would be warm inside; the sweet heat would nourish their tired souls.

Bin and Churl walked the horses to the rear of the building and wrestled with the icy door of the stable. Once inside they closed the stubborn door because the area was moderately heated and they did not want the precious commodity to escape. They hung the saddles on hooks and brushed away the snow and ice that had hung in frozen clumps from the poor horses. Oats, water and fresh straw . . . . The horses would be fine. A door on the opposite side of the stable promised to lead into the main building.

Carlotta and Quay'Sea entered the front door and were immediately greeted with a voice yelling, "Close the door". Big Ben stood by the bar and although his voice was harsh, his smile welcomed his new visitors. This was more than a trading post, it was a lodge. Ben came over and shook hands with Quay'Sea and gave Carlotta a tilt of his shaggy head. Ben explained that his northern outpost was the last place where comforts could be enjoyed. He offered rooms, hot food, libation and various goods. Carlotta informed Ben that their two companions were stabling the horses and would soon join them. They all required rooms and hot food but what they needed even more was information.

Ben enjoyed visitors, especially those who had travelled a long distance; they carried news from the south. Ben promised that he and his wife would dine with them and provide any information that they could but first they needed to clean up, warm up and rest. Bin and Churl burst through the stable's side door and, after brief introductions, Ben showed all of them to cozy rooms located above the kitchen. These were the warmest rooms at the lodge. Ben intended to go to the kitchen himself and spit a lamb which would be ready to feed his party when they woke. Helga would take care of baking some fresh loaves to sop up the fat and juices.

In her room, a small boy appeared and served Carlotta a jug of hot mead. While she warmed her insides, he delivered bucketfuls of steaming water which he unceremoniously pored into a large baliya, a metal bath tub, which sat in the centre of the room. Big Ben knew what his guests needed. Once the baliya was almost full, the boy presented Carlotta with towels and a small vial of sweet smelling oil before he ran off to his next chore. With her door firmly bolted to avoid interruption, Carlotta stripped off her damp garments and sank into the rough baliya. The experience was better than any of the fancy baths she had ever taken back at home. The aromatic oil relaxed her further and made this bath feel like paradise; she would soak her tired bones as long as the water retained its heat. The time passed too quickly for Carlotta and soon she dried her body and slipped naked into the inviting feather bed that had been heated with some warm rocks. What seemed like only moments later, Quay'Sea was knocking on her door to call her for the evening meal.

Ben and Helga were very attentive hosts; the meal was spectacular and the guests were dually impressed. A feast in the wasteland . . . . The lamb was juicy and cooked to perfection. Helga's potatoes and fresh bread, both generously spread with soft butter tasted like bliss. Ben regaled the group with stories about his daughter and the merriment he had experienced with her when she was growing up in this remote area. Quays and Carlotta listened and were infected with Ben's delight and joy when he spoke of his sweet Lily.

Completely sated, it was time for Quays to ask the questions they had come to pose. Quays described Den and Carl but Ben assured them that no one of that description had come through The Bay of Glaciers recently. Recently? Quays asked if anyone had ever travelled this way, who did look like one of the men that he described. As it happened, several months ago, a young girl had come through with a group of rowdy hooligans. Ben was pleased to see them go; they had created an atmosphere that was not to Ben's liking. The girl Ben remembered had been frail and seemed worn out by her journey. She must have come a long way but neither she nor the men spoke about where they came from. Her complexion was chalky and her hair was a mass of raven curls that fell almost to her waist. She had a far away look; like someone suffering from the after effects of imbibing too much mead. The group had stayed only one night and appeared to have taken the coast trail toward Bluff Bay but Ben could not really be sure of their intended destination. He explained that Bluff Bay was nothing more than a group of natives who lived off what little this land had to offer. They bred dogs that they used for pulling their sleds. Ben had a team of dogs and a sled that he had traded for when the natives last visited Glacier Bay for a few supplies. He rarely saw these elusive people but always welcomed them when they chose to come and trade their furs and skins.

Carlotta and Quay'Sea's minds were both working to capacity. This had to have been Fannie that Ben described. This meant that they were on the right track but they both wondered why Den and Carl had not visited The Bay of Glaciers. They quizzed Ben relentlessly; eventually they needed one important question answered. How could one travel north from The Bay of Glaciers? They needed to go further into this uninviting land to catch up with their human quarry. Ben was an empathic individual and he registered that the girl he had mentioned was important to these travellers. They seemed like good people, he would help them in any way that he could.

There were really only two ways to travel north from The Bay of Glaciers. One could follow the shores of the bay to the inlet at Bluff Bay where a northerly course could be resumed and followed all the way to North Point. Less used and a somewhat unreliable second choice was to travel by sea. The fishers from the north occasionally sailed into The Bay of Glaciers to drop off supplies of frozen whale meat and sheets of crudely cured hide that they stripped from the sea beasts they harvested. They also traded in frozen fish which they scooped from the sea with their cleverly designed nets. In the north, they traded exclusively with Ben, who had the means to keep the fish frozen in a shallow cellar. They enjoyed his hospitality for days on end when they chose to visit. Travellers could pay for passage with these friendly fishers but one never knew when they would choose to arrive or when they would choose to leave. This did not appear to Quay'Sea to be a very reliable means of travel but if the fishers chose to present themselves within the next few days he would consider it.

CHAPTER 29

THE HALLWAY WAS drafty and very cold. Den kept his coat tightly wrapped but let his hood drop down his back. He wasn't sure exactly how to proceed; he needed to get inside the castle but he had to be stealthy. The passageways below this castle were like the labyrinth on The Society's grounds except here it was dark. He held out his hand and concentrated till a tiny flame appeared and hovered over his palm. It would suffice to see where he was going but he had to be careful not to pass the place where Carl was incapacitated. If he had regained consciousness, this small flame would be all that he would need to incite an inferno that could engulf the entire labyrinth.

Den knew that he could easily be disoriented if he lost rack of the turns he made. The walls were all caked with salt residue and he decided to use his small blade to leave inconspicuous marks to be sure he wasn't confused into backtracking. Den's stomach grumbled with hunger, he must have been lost in this maze for hours. He had yet to pass one of his markings so he pushed on hoping to find an entrance into the castle itself. When he finally reached the centre of the maze, he became disillusioned when all he could see was a stone bench sitting on a raised dais. He scanned and then meticulously searched the ceiling and the floor for hidden trapdoors to no avail. He was hungry, cold and trapped in a labyrinth that he had entered of his own accord. What kind of a hero had he turned out to be? His sister was a captive in the castle above and he had made himself a prisoner below.

He sat down on the bench and it immediately began to move. The solid rock ceiling silently slid aside and the dais began to rise up. Den sat and watched as he rose into a room that looked much like the catacombs below except for the salty residue. Here the walls were roughly honed granite with no apparent joints. Den marvelled at the sheer size of the rock that must have been used to craft this room. He was inside the castle but he reasoned that it was not an inhabited area because it was unheated and dark. There were four exits from this room, none of which were barred. He still carried his flame and walked around the room peering into each of the exits. They all looked exactly the same so he randomly chose a doorway and stepped out of the room. The moment he entered the hallway, the doorways all sealed and Den could hear the dais moving back down into the labyrinth. There would be no chance of returning this way so Den did the only thing left to him; he slowly and quietly walked along the hallway. Wall sconces and torches hung on the walls so Den took a torch and lit it so he could extinguish his magical flame. He didn't want to have to explain his gifts if he encountered someone who lived in the castle.

Hallways led to stairways and more hallways with large rooms, none of which were decorated. Den wondered if anyone actually lived here. He turned a corner and realized that he was entering another maze. He was backing out when he heard footsteps fast approaching. He turned and found himself looking up into the face of a very tall young man. The youth did not look at all surprised to have met Den in this remote location so Den behaved as though he belonged here. He wasn't sure how to reply when he was asked if he was heading to the library. The young man introduced himself as Shilinar B'Edard and asked Den if he was newly arrived. Den decided to play along as well as he could and introduced himself and admitted that he was new and apparently lost. Shilinar laughed out loud and told Den to follow him. He wanted to go into the library first but as soon as he returned his book and chose another, he was heading to the mess. This idea of food suited Den but he was quite nervous about openly walking around the castle.

Shilinar led Den through the labyrinth with ease and they soon arrived in the cavernous library. Shilinar replaced the book he had been carrying and chose an ancient looking text which he put under his arm. With a smile, he beckoned Den to follow and they were on their way to have a meal.

Den did not look at all out of the ordinary wearing his heavy outer garments. It seemed that everybody he passed was bundled up against the severe cold. There was no heat at all in this stone fortress. He followed closely behind Shilinar and soon found himself in a room where numerous men and women were sitting on large granite chairs drinking hot tea and eating food that smelled wonderful. Shilinar placed the text he was carrying into his deep pocket and pointed Den toward a chair. They both sat and were immediately served a hot brew that was not exactly tea but it made Den's insides happy. Shilinar spoke quietly to the server and then leaned toward Den and apologized for just having delayed their evening meal. He wanted to wait for his friends to arrive so that they could all eat together.

Fannie and Mushy were engaged in an animated conversation as they entered the mess hall and automatically made their way toward their usual table. Den had his back to them but Shilinar saw them coming and waved them over. When Den saw Shilinar wave he turned in his chair and locked eyes with Fannie.

It was only once he saw them together that Shilly's mind started connecting the evidence and he wondered if this wanderer, which he had rescued in the bowels of the Enclave, was somehow related to Fannie. They shared the same complexion and hair colour but the main thing that was now quite obvious, was their eyes. They had exactly the same extraordinary eyes.

Fannie dropped her barrier and flung her mind at Den. They communed for only a few moments and exchanged all that had occurred in their lives since they had been torn apart. Fannie also conveyed the urgency to leave this crowded area before somebody noticed that Den did not really belong. They had not yet uttered a single word but they were already formulating a plan to keep Den hidden. Before she left his mind she warned him to erect a barrier and to open his thoughts to no one.

The moments that Fannie and Den spent, seemingly awestruck with each other, were awkward for Shilly and Mushy. They had never seen Fannie react this way to anybody and Mushy was especially concerned because he had never seen this young man before. Fannie asked Shilly if he would bring all of their meals up to her chamber where they could all enjoy their repast in a quiet and private place. Shilly instantly agreed and a confused Mushy just shook his head and tagged along to help Shilly carry the trays.

Fannie walked calmly out of the mess with Den following closely behind. They did not appear to be walking together so as not to attract any attention. Only after they both entered Fannie's room and secured the door were they able to fall into each others arms and hold one another while silent tears of relief ran down their cheeks. Den told Fannie how impressed he was with her powers. Now that he was educated, he could recognise her gifts when he entered her mind. Fannie also held a new respect for her brother because his gifts were numerous and his power was vast. Best of all, they were together and fate would not be so cruel as to put them together just to have them fail to escape this place.

Den now knew everything that Fannie knew, so he was familiar with the Enclave and its master Vigour. He knew Mushy and Shilly as though they had been his friends for a long time. He knew how Fannie felt about the boys and he realized that they would have to be included in any plan to escape. Fannie explained why it was unwise to confide any plans to the boys because V could enter minds that were not schooled to erect barriers. They couldn't even tell the boys about Den's true identity for fear that V would somehow find out. This was going to be difficult but Fannie believed that she and Den could overcome any obstacles now that they were together.

CHAPTER 30

QUAY'SEA AND CARLOTTA sat in front of the huge fireplace in Ben's common room trying to decide what their next course of action should be. The brutal winds battered against the sturdy log walls of the lodge to add to the stranded and desolate feelings that were threatening to overwhelm Carlotta and were definitely affecting Quays. They had sent their last pigeon, with a message, back at the crossroad so they were on their own in the far north. If they were to be lost, no one would know where they went and what had happened to them. Carlotta confided that she was worried about what they were racing to face and Quays added his concern about their ability to survive the elements in this inhospitable environment. In addition, they were responsible for the welfare of their two charges and this duty weighed heavily upon both Society members.

As it happened, the weather broke and provided a short respite from the constant wind. The icy temperatures were bearable and almost pleasant when the wind remained calm and abated its constant blowing of snow and frozen pellets into one's face. This was the sign that Quays had been waiting for. They could probably make Bluff Bay in a three day walk using the cleverly designed snow hikers that Ben was willing to provide. The woven, tear drop shaped, apparatus were strapped to one's boots and distributed body weight over a larger area to keep the walker on the snow's surface. Once a person adjusted his gait, the snow walkers were a practical way to move easily on the feathery snow surface. The horses would have to stay here in the stables because no fanciful creation had been invented to keep these heavy beasts from plunging through the snow. Bin and Churl were outdoors in the wooded area chopping out the deadwood that would provide fodder for Ben's fireplaces. They worked to help pay Ben for his hospitality but Quays also had one of the silver pieces, with which he had been entrusted, reserved for Ben and Helga to thank them for their generosity and for the information they had imparted. While the fair weather held, it was time to push forth in the hopes that they could all arrive at their next destination intact and unharmed.

After a hearty morning meal, the four travellers made ready to depart The Bay of Glaciers. Ben had convinced them not only to use the snow walkers but to take the dogs and sled along to stow their gear and make their walk easier. Bin and Churl were preparing the sled outside the most remote shed when they spied a ship out in the sea. They ran to get Ben and he brought his spy glass to better see the ship that was still a distant speck on the icy bay.

The fishers had experienced the best luck. On their way back to Ice Port, after dropping their passengers at the dreaded castle, they were carefully making their way between the floating bergs on The Bay of Ice. A school of whales had passed directly through their path and the fishers took advantage of the available bounty. They filled their icy hold with slabs of whale meat and huge lumps of delicious fat. For the fishers, this was as good a reason as any to visit Ben and enjoy a few days of Helga's fine cooking. When they docked at The Bay of Glaciers, they would be able to drop their wooden traps into the shallows and collect the colossal lagostra, which were plentiful at this time of year. Like giant spiders of the sea, these huge creatures could be as large as a child. They were only ever known to crawl along the bottom of the shallows in The Bay of Glaciers. These delicacies could be frozen and would eventually demand a pretty coin when they ultimately made their way back to The Port of Merle.

Ben entered the lodge and excitedly informed Carlotta and Quay'Sea that the fishers had arrived. They were anchoring their vessel and readying the small dinghies that would be used to bring the crew on shore. Fate had intervened once again and their journey north would be eased; the trip would be much faster and more comfortable aboard the fisher's barge. They would save days of travel, by avoiding the long walk southwest just to round the Bluff. The punishing east coast of Afshen would have to wait for other brave souls to face its gauntlet of icy winds, blowing snow and fearsome creatures like the great white bear.

The fishers had been blessed with fair weather as they disembarked their vessel and rowed through calm waters to reach Ben's small dock. As they boisterously entered the lodge, they brought their fishy and musky stench with them. Helga was already preparing to launder and freshen their clothing while the errand boy and his partner ran up the stairs with numerous bucketfuls of steaming water. The baliyas were being filled and scented with sweet oils. These swarthy and rugged men of the sea still took moments to enjoy the finer things that life had to offer; one of these things was a bath, at least once or twice a year, and another was the cuisine from

Helga's kitchen. A small stuffed pig was already beginning to defrost in a tub by the fire and it would soon be sizzling over the hearth, ready to feed the guests this delicacy which they rarely enjoyed. Potatoes were oiled, wrapped in spiced vine leaves and buried in the banked embers of the fire to roast slowly. Helga was busy in the kitchen, kneading the dough that would be shaped into long trenchers and baked, to be served hot to scoop up the juicy pork. A feast was in the making and Quays and Carlotta had new plans to devise. Their first step would be to approach the fishers to attempt to gain passage on the ship, and the rest would have to be left to fate. It was mid afternoon and Carlotta retired to her room to rest and Quays dozed contentedly by the fire.

Vlad was the captain of the trawler and he came to sit with Quay'Sea by the fire in the common room to await the hot dinner that was nearly ready. After they exchanged brief introductions, Quays informed Vlad of his need to book passage on Vlad's ship. Vlad laughed and enquired about where exactly Quays thought he wanted to go. He wouldn't be heading back toward The Port of Merle for at least a half season. The hold of his ship needed to be filled before the trip would be viable. Quays assured the captain that he wanted to go north. Vlad counselled that the far north offered little in the way of comforts and people could not survive the climate. Where would his group find shelter? Vlad had no wish to abandon four individuals to the harsh wasteland. He explained that he was already experiencing enough guilt over leaving two boys in a dinghy on the rough coast at North Point. His dreams had been haunted by visions of the two young lads floating frozen among the bergs. He had no intention of stranding four more people to meet their doom.

Two young men? This captain had ferried and delivered two young men to North Point? Excitement sparked and built within Quay'Sea. Without appearing daft, Quay'Sea hurriedly explained that it was a pair of young boys he was searching for. This was the only reason that his group was travelling north. If the captain could bring them to the place where the boys had last been seen, he was prepared to pay 2 silvers. The captain's eyes gleamed at the offer; 2 silvers were more than the price an entire shipment delivered to Port of Merle paid. The deal was struck, Quays handed Vlad 1 silver now and promised the second when they arrived at their destination. The men shook hands to seal the deal.

Quay'Sea rushed up the stairs to rouse Carlotta and inform her of their new plan. She was very excited but concerned that they had no pigeon to send to let Morgan know where the boys were. Not that anyone could arrive in this remote location in time to lend support but at least he would have known where they were and what was happening.

The fishers stayed at The Bay of Glaciers for only 2 days because their new passengers were so anxious to be on their way. Quay'Sea took Vlad aside and informed him that his group of travellers were magicians. Quays did not want to surprise Vlad and their crew when and if they witnessed him or the boys using their gifts. Quays foresaw the possibility and probably the necessity to use his skills, especially when they were disembarking the ship in the rough sea. Vlad was not a superstitious man except for his firm belief in fate. In fact, in the past, Vlad had hired gifted individuals who could affect the weather to voyage with him into especially dangerous waters. Vlad divulged that he believed that the castle at North Point was a place of magic. Quays was not surprised and was actually quite sure that whoever inhabited that castle was a very powerful magician or sorcerer. Quays would find more than he had bargained for once he reached the Enclave.

The day they departed Glacier The Bay of Glaciers, Ben asked Carlotta to deliver a package to his daughter, Lily. She lived in the area of North Point with her husband, Vigour. He was a quiet man who made a good life for their daughter in such a barren wasteland. He had stayed at The Bay of Glaciers for some time and when he moved north, Lily went with him. Ben confided that he had communicated by sending letters and packages for a few years. He and Helga were grandparents to 2 sets of twins that they had never met. They were unable to leave the lodge and Lily was not able to travel such a distance with 4 children. Of late, they had not heard from her and they were worried. Carlotta promised to deliver the package if she was able.

The weather was bleak as the dinghies were rowed back and forth to load all the fishers and the passengers onto the ship. Ice pellets were sweeping across the frothy sea causing a layer of ice to form on the surfaces of the deck and the mast. The Captain was eager to get under way so they delayed only long enough to pull up the lagostra traps and subdue the spindly creatures until they froze solid. With the catch stowed in a cold compartment, the passengers were asked to remain below while the sailors did their jobs. They would reach North Point within 5 days so long as the wind stayed with them.

CHAPTER 31

V AND MOIRA HAD been extremely occupied planning the expansion of their sphere of influence. The northern Enclave was built for one reason only; to collect and train minions who could be sent forth to do V's bidding. The membership of the Enclave had expanded to such a degree that V believed that the day he had been anticipating had arrived. He trusted that he had the power, and the accoutrements, to rule his own kingdom and his trained subordinates were prepared to go out and begin collecting territory for their master. V's thirst for domination was expanding exponentially and Moira fed his obsession because she anticipated maintaining her station as "the woman behind the man". Together, they listed all their members and their gifts, which were a part of the Enclave's arsenal, which were now available for V's use in a campaign to implement his own agenda. V intended to send out his membership, one to each small town in an ever increasing radius, and to threaten the citizens with repercussions if they chose to defy his rule. They would begin with the north but V's real interest lay further south. He wanted authority over the entire northern continent; he aimed to become the king of Adnil.

V determined that his perfect world would be one where he could comfortably travel his domain and have his subjects worship and pay homage to him. He had chilling plans for Adnil that would ensure that the people obeyed and feared their new self appointed King.

V had been so involved with Moira, scheming and preparing the spells and incantations he would use in the first phase of his strategy that he had overlooked the events that were taking place beneath his own roof. He had given up in his attempts to infiltrate Fannie's mind but he often visited Bardook's thoughts to keep abreast of Fannie's progress. He hadn't entered Mushy's mind since he had found the nugget of immorality that had convinced him to begin Fannie's education and had left Mushy a mental mess for almost a fortnight. With all the gifts being used in the Enclave, a magical current always seemed to be running through the structure itself.

Each member, candidate and novice practiced the magical arts on a daily basis so V couldn't possibly keep track of each individual spell or the use of power. V's distraction with Moira and the overwhelming use of the arts combined to keep Den's arrival at the Enclave a secret. Had Den arrived earlier in the season when there were fewer inhabitants at the Enclave, V would certainly have registered the powers Den used in the catacombs against his traitorous enemy, Carl.

Fannie still had to attend her lessons with Bardook and make appearances in the mess so as not to attract attention. Late each night, hidden in her room, Fannie and Den shared one mind where they tried to determine how best to escape their circumstances. Connected as they were, they noticed a new sensation between them that felt like a tingling. It was almost like there was a separate presence communing with them when they were sharing a connection. Neither of them registered any sense of the indefinable spectre when they were behind their own personal barriers, only when they were joined. This presented a mystery which they would have to solve eventually but for the moment, they had more pressing issues.

Mushy accepted Den as a newly arrived novice but Shilly furtively believed that Den was either Fannie's brother or at least a close relative. Shilly was more intuitive than Fannie suspected and his suspicions were beginning to include his belief that Fannie and Den were planning to leave the Enclave. This thought bothered Shilly because he cared for Fannie and worried that she would end up frozen and probably dead if she left the security of the castle to attempt a futile escape with this young man who was just as frail as Fannie herself. What Shilly didn't suspect was the power young Den could wield. He also didn't know how much talent Fannie had discovered in herself since Bardook had been cultivating her skills. Shilly surreptitiously pledged that he would attempt to aid Fannie's escape if this was what she wished. He only hoped that he and Mushy could join the couple when they attempted their getaway because he was beginning to feel that he and his jolly friend did not belong in this place. Those individuals who were most successful and revered at this Enclave were hateful, arrogant, greedy, dishonest and evil. Shilly was literally afraid of most of his colleagues.

Ten days had passed since Shilly had found Den in the catacombs. Carl may be dead or he may well have escaped his frozen bonds by now and be wandering the labyrinth below the castle. He may have even made his way into the Enclave and reported Den's arrival to his master. Den felt an irresistible urge to implement the only escape strategy that he and Fannie had been able to devise. They knew that they had magic at their disposal to help them survive the elements outside the castle but they had to somehow escape the castle undetected, to maintain a covert posture from the multitude of individuals in this building who could almost certainly overpower and defeat them in a magical battle.

CHAPTER 32

JUST BEFORE EVENING meal was to be served, Den and Fannie collected Mushy and Shilly and suggested an exploration of the outer walls of the castle. After some convincing, they set off, dressed more warmly that usual because it was always coldest in close proximity to the exterior walls. Shilly was not surprised when Den led them out through an exit but Mushy was perturbed because many who had left the castle had never returned. It was forbidden to venture outdoors without permission from one's mentor or a member. Shilly did his best to convince Mushy to remain calm and trust Fannie and Den. Reluctantly, Mushy cooperated and took Shilly's advice. Shilly inferred that this was the escape he had been expecting and he was most appreciative to have been included. The four escapees circled the perimeter of the Enclave until Den got his bearings and guided them across an expanse of barren snow toward a huge rock, behind which he had stowed the dinghy which he and Carl had used when they had arrived ten days earlier. It was a long run from the wall to the rock, and they would be visible from the castle, in the unlikely circumstance, that someone happened to be looking out a window.

At dusk, V and Moira stood outdoors, on the top of the highest tower of the Enclave. Moira had spent the entire day artistically recreating the signatures that V would need to cast his spell. The rocky floor of the tower was completely covered with runes and symbols, completely encircling the statue of dear Lily. V stood at ease in the freezing temperatures, dressed in clothing anyone else would have chosen to wear on a warm spring day, while Moira was bundled up against the bitter cold. From this vantage point, they could peruse the horizon in any and all directions. V's attention was drawn toward the south. He was slowly gathering his powers and concentrating on the task at hand. Moira stood patiently in the doorway that led to the only staircase which descended the tower. V stepped cautiously between the signatures which enabled his powers to grow and coalesce around his person. Moira knew that he was almost ready for the casting. She glanced around to be sure that all the conditions were exactly right when she glimpsed a spec on the eastern horizon. A fisher's barge was making its way toward the Point, probably on its way to Port Merle. She dared not disturb V at this critical juncture in his incantation so she kept her eyes on the spec as it slowly grew to confirm that it was, in fact, just a fisher's barge that was probably steering its course a little close to shore, but not anything to be concerned about.

V gathered his energy and literally sizzled with power. He raised his arms so that both of his hands pointed south and began to chant the incantation that would be enhanced by the power signatures laid at his feet. His concentration was of paramount importance because this spell was complex and aimed at the manipulation of the climate. Rings of vibration emanated from the tips of V's fingers, and a blue luminosity oozed from his eyes and down his body. The blue radiance crawled over the signatures and down the outside of the castle where it seemed to flow like tiny waterways toward the south. All the while, V pulsed with power, emitting more of the vibrating rings which also travelled south but through the air itself. From the corner of his eye, V was momentarily distracted by four dark flecks, on the white expanse of snow, moving quickly away from the castle. It wasn't much of a disturbance but it was enough to disrupt V's concentration and the spell began to falter. V roared with exasperation but all was not lost; most of his spell had been cast, the distraction had only caused it to be less potent so its effect would not be as devastating as V had originally planned. V was infuriated and he aimed his mind at the four who had disturbed his conjuring; they would pay for being outdoors. He was momentarily baffled when he was unable to enter all four minds but everything became clear when he entered Shilly's thoughts. They were attempting an escape and his ridiculous friend, Mushy, was running with them. The best news of all was that Fannie and her brother were the ones leading this futile flight. Where did they think they could run? Finally, V had both of the twins. This was turning out to be an excellent day, even if his insidious spell had been diminished, it had not been extinguished.

V stood at the very edge of the tower and when he spoke, his voice was projected toward the four fleeing individuals. It was so loud it caused the small pieces of ice to reverberate in Den's path. V's words echoed in Shilly's and Mushy's unprotected minds. V was laughing and mocking their futile efforts; he spewed out warnings to the group which instructed them to immediately return to the castle to avoid harsh punishment. Fannie helped Mushy and Den assisted Shilly to keep running toward the rock. V's mind was incapacitating the boys and making it difficult for them to run, even with help. If they didn't comply with V's commands, he would soon choose another weapon from his arsenal of power to stop them. The boys couldn't go on and fell to the ground, writhing in pain inflicted through the mind link that V established.

Fannie and Den tried to pull the boys along but they were just too heavy for the fragile twins. Fannie stood and turned to face the castle. She glared up at the tower where V was leering at the four interlopers. He was in a good position to use his gifts because he still stood on the tower floor where the signatures would amplify his powers. Den followed his sister's example and stood beside her protecting the boys from any harm that V may inflict. V's maniacal laughter echoed off the very surface of the hard packed ice. The reverberations caused some of the large flat pieces of ice to crack and collapse inward, causing small earthquakes around the shivering group on the surface. The shaking and rocking caused Fannie to land hard on her backside but she never broke her gaze with V. With their mind barriers in place, Fannie and Den were not linked with each other. They did not want to give V an opportunity to enter either of their minds. Den stepped closer to Fannie but she did not accept any assistance; she stood and with an obstinate look she cast a thought at V. She was attempting to control his judgement and the suggestion she planted in the recesses of his mind encouraged him to leave them to their own fate in this barren land. She was a clever girl who knew that V would never allow them to escape but the image of the four freezing and dying delinquents was pleasing to V. He could not allow these twins to abandon his dominion and remain free or alive to assist his enemies in the south.

Fannie was working hard inside her own mind. She had practiced partitioning her mind with Bardook and now the opportunity to use her skill had presented itself. She thought of the most insignificant details of her life on the farm with El. Images of chopping vegetables and singing songs with the children were arranged as a neat obstruction in the forefront of her mind. Into this safe enclosure, she would invite V to pay a quick visit. She had been able to contain Bardook with only a fraction of her power so she was confident that she could hold V at bay while reading his thoughts and plans. She and Den needed to understand why they were so significant to this master of the Enclave.

V aimed his right arm at the four icebound individuals and blasted them with a vibrating force that knocked Den and Fannie flat and rattled their very bones. Fannie regained her composure, sat up and sent V a hint of an opening in her mind. His reaction was instantaneous; he leapt into her mind, intending to gain complete control of Fannie. He was momentarily baffled and very promptly infuriated when he determined that she had him enclosed in an area where he could learn little and venture nowhere. V used the power enhancing signatures at his disposal to appraise the barrier he faced in an effort to find a weakness where he could aim his attack. In the moments while this exchange took place, Den gathered his strength and caused the mild winds to blow with a greater intensity. V's clothing flapped in the strong wind that was reaching hurricane force at the top of the tower. His hair swirled and pulled away from the clasp which had held it neatly at the nape of his neck. The clasp flew from the tower and as V grabbed for it, he caught his finger in the leather thong which kept his amber amulet around his neck. The amulet, fashioned by Moira, which had hung around V's neck to disguise his disfigurement, was detached and lost to the strong winds. V was enraged and looked around to find Moira. She was nowhere to be seen. He cast his mind to search for her and found her fleeing down the long dark staircase. She would pay for deserting him and attempting to flee to save herself. V used his mind to physically push Moira into the wall where she instantly became frozen in place. Moira knew what fate awaited her and she screamed in agony as V slowly let her suffer her immortalisation. She would decorate the wall of the staircase just as Lily decorated the top of the tower. Not one iota of compassion existed in V, he smiled as he felt her suffering and he was pleased with the agonizing look on her face that was now permanently etched into place.

V returned his attention to the matters at hand. He raised his arms and caused himself to levitate and move out over the precipice of the tower's edge. He lowered himself to the icy facade to stand and face Fannie and Den. The boys were incapacitated but conscious, lying on the cracked surface but no longer writhing in pain. Den's wind had been allowed to subside and the three adversaries faced each other on that calm and bitter evening on V's frozen home turf.

V was intrigued by the twins' confidence when they faced him. His newly visible scarred visage was daunting in itself but also, Fannie was well aware of the powers that V could wield. He decided that he would toy with them and make an effort to convince them to join his cause but if they proved too stubborn, he would destroy them. They would make beautiful effigies to be added to his growing collection of castle adornments. When he finally broke the silence, V insisted that the twins come back to the castle and be welcomed into his fold. They would be well treated and their stations would be high in the succession of the membership. Den smirked and his look was enough for V to see that his generous offer had been rejected. Fannie was not showing any signs of acceptance but V held out hope, knowing that she possessed a shred of the evil he had searched for. V aimed his first attack at Den, if he couldn't have them both, he wanted Fannie alive.

Before he could react, Den found himself frozen in place in the icy surface. He immediately exuded heat and regained his readiness. The next wave of power hit him and the vibration promised to shake his bones apart. Fannie sent a rain of sharp ice pellets at V, aimed at his ruined face. This distraction gave Den the moment he needed to repel V's vibrating spell. From his education, Den knew that he needed to use a gift against V that V himself did not possess. This would make it more difficult for V to defend himself thus causing him to use his power more unreservedly. If he could be weakened or incapacitated, the foursome could still manage an escape. V used the cold when he cast spells and he chose to live where it was cold. Den decided to test V's abilities with fire. Den held up his palm and chanted for a flame to appear. Several tiny flickers appeared and Den fuelled them with power till they coalesced and swelled into a substantial ball of liquid fire. He hurled this weapon at V who reacted quickly enough to stop most of the fire from reaching him. The few liquid particles that clung to V's hands and arms did considerable damage and caused V to howl in pain. Apparently, V had no power to extinguish fire although he may well be able to manipulate it. Fannie and Den both determined, as one, that they had found V's Achilles heel. Fannie used her powers to enfold herself, Den and the boys in a large bubble of heat. The relief from the bitter cold was anathema and caused V to step back. V was enraged and tried to attack Fannie's mind to banish this foreign heat that did not belong in his realm. Her barriers were impenetrable and this only served to infuriate V further. He triggered the rubble and boulders which littered the coast to fly at Fannie and Den but Den's dominion over all things earthly allowed him to cause the debris to hold and hover in place, never reaching its intended target. All the while, V was casting a spell to encapsulate himself against another attack of fire. A crackling icy bubble, appeared around the sorcerer, which would repel any further sparks or flames. V hovered, a full body length above the glacial ground, and glared at his quarry.

The boys had regained their strength and were backing their way toward the shelter of the large boulder on the beach. Fannie and Den stayed close to the boys and kept themselves between V and their friends. It was at this moment that V noticed a small dinghy being tossed in the surf just beyond the beachhead. A man and a woman were using magic and doing their best to calm the breakers to help propel their small craft to the shore. Den and Fannie turned to see what had drawn V's attention. Den recognised Quay'Sea and Carlotta and he waved for them to approach the beach. Den raised his hand to be ready to deflect any spell that V might throw toward his friends. Within their haven of heat, Den, Fannie, Mushy and Shilly made their way behind the boulder and found the derelict dinghy that Den and Carl had stashed for their escape.

V shot a bolt of ice toward Quay'Sea's small craft but Den deflected its course and the tiny boat landed safely on the pebbled and ice encrusted shore. The group of six needed time to escape and Den could only think of one way to provide it. He stood in deep concentration. He would utilize all of his power in this one gambit to facilitate their final escape. A red tinged circle began to radiate from Den's body and its diameter grew as it flowed over the ground. The group of six were inside the circle and as it grew, it melted the ice and left a warm air inside its circumference. As it expanded toward V, he backed away, as from an open flame. The circle continued to expand at a growing rate until V and his entire castle were inside its heated environment. V kept himself safe inside his personal bubble but as he watched, his castle began to list on its foundation. V had to turn his entire attention to saving his Enclave. He used considerable power to expand his personal bubble to encase his home and keep it properly frozen in place. Den was exhausted and couldn't have used his magic to accomplish even the most mundane action. Quay'Sea and Carlotta helped Fannie to load the group into a dinghy and they made their way through the calmed waters toward the fishers' barge. Den's magic circle of heat would keep V's attention and efforts occupied for days. He would be severely weakened by the effort it would cost him to put his realm back to the way he desired. Thanks to Den, they had the time they needed to make their escape.

CHAPTER 33

THEY ALL SAT huddled together, below decks, on the fishers' barge as it made its way south toward The Port of Merle. The fishers were happy to take the passengers south when Quay'Sea offered to double their fee. They rode high in the water as they ploughed their way south, with an empty hold which the fishers could now well afford to fill with goods for their return trip. Den remained weak and would require some time to recover from his colossal use of power. Fannie joined with her weakened brother and funnelled some of her power into him to ease his convalescence. He quickly regained his composure and the group spent many hours chatting and acquainting and reacquainting themselves with each other. Quay'Sea assured Mushy and Shilly that they would be welcomed by The Society and that they would be given the opportunity to explore their gifts. Carlotta regaled them with stories about her favourite places on the grounds around the palace till Shilly and Mushy were more excited than she was to arrive at their destination. Den and Fannie were the only two who fully appreciated the threat that V continued to pose. When Fannie had entered V's mind, just before the battle at North Point, she had become privy to all of his insidious plans. She knew his strengths and his weakness but worst of all she knew about the spell he had cast from the tower before he had been interrupted by their escape. Den now knew everything his sister knew and together they decided to share the information with the chancellor at The Society before they shared it with anybody else. They were plagued with worry about V's spell and what intensity he had managed to instil in his hex before the casting. They did not relish facing this adversary who had most certainly become their personal enemy but they knew that fate surely meant for their paths to cross once more.

After 7 days of sailing south along the Madyar coast, the vessel docked at the port and the eight friends were more than ready to make their way home. Den led the group to the inn where he had stabled Dash and Carl's stallion, Brock. They took rooms and spent the rest of the day readying the supplies they would require for the 5 or 6 day journey back to Manek.

They would require four more horses for their passage and poor Carlotta, once again, would rely on Quays' magic to calm her dreadful symptoms as she rode home. Bin and Churl were anxious to return to The Society where they will have gained new notoriety just by accompanying Quay'Sea and Carlotta on this successful rescue mission. They planned to regale the other candidates with tales from the north that would keep them rapt for days. Quays felt that the twins were keeping something from him. He was eager to arrive within the safe walls of the palace so that he could speak his concerns to Morgan. Quays trusted Den and Fannie but he was worried that the news they carried back to Manek would not ease his mind. Fannie felt as though she already knew The Society even though she had never been there nor had she met any of the members, other than the four who had helped with the harrowing escape. Den remained connected to Fannie on a consistent basis so she had time to revisit all of the memories of his short stay in the palace and his education regarding all things magical. She had always looked up to her brother but now she was in awe of his gifts and talents. Den considered Fannie's newly discovered gifts superior to his own. He could affect fire, water, air and earth and he could communicate with Fannie through their shared mind link but Den believed that Fannie was responsible for the link's existence. Den's ability to communicate and search the minds of others was a weak gift compared to Fannie's. Even before she was tutored, Fannie had been able to commune with El, who had no magical gifts. Bardook may have been V's minion but he had proved to be a nurturing teacher and he had schooled Fannie with a tempered hand. She was well acquainted with her abilities; she had yet to appreciate the considerable power she could wield.

They had to remain vigilant for anything that may appear out of the ordinary because they knew that V would not rest for very long. He may be sending out spells or webs to hamper their trek. Quay'Sea believed that V's recovery would probably take longer that Den's had taken. V was left to deal with Den's spell which threatened to melt the very foundation of his castle Enclave. It was uncertain how long V had to labour to save the structure that Den had so aptly threatened. Once recovered, V's powers would rank him as a powerful adversary and his defeat at the foot of his own home, would serve to make him an embittered enemy.

The group of eight rode out of The Port of Merle headed into the sunrise, anticipating fair weather to begin the final leg of their passage home. The men were all accustomed to riding horseback but Fannie and Carlotta felt the body aches associated with riding for hours. They stopped often to massage their sore muscles until suddenly, Fannie's mind was filled with Carlotta's pain. Her immediate reaction was to send healing sensations into Carlotta and to speak an ancient word that conjured relaxation. Her own pain had not triggered a magical response but the suffering of another had caused Fannie to react with her compassionate healing skills. Once connected, Fannie searched Carlotta's physical being and calmed her adverse reaction brought on by animal dander. Carlotta would never again suffer from being in close proximity to a four legged creature. All the while, Den was linked with Fannie and he was most impressed with her abilities. Her empathy for others was a virtue that would make her especially welcomed by The Society. Inspired by her work with Carlotta, Fannie treated her own sore muscles and the group was able to make better time.

At dusk, they found a sheltered spot close to a fast moving creek where they stopped for the night and their evening meal. The horses were being tended by Bin and Churl while the two Society members sat with Den and Fannie, close to the fire. It was unseasonably chilly and the fire felt good, especially after all the freezing temperatures they had all recently endured. Bin was the first to raise an alarm. He and Churl were soaking their tired feet in the creek when flashes of blue light streaked through the water. Den and Fannie led the way and Quay'Sea and Carlotta followed directly when the boys began shouting their distress. When the four arrived, they witnessed the alien blue flashes which moved like startled fishes just below the surface of the moving water. Fannie was the first to identify the apparitions; these were V's creations which were travelling south to carry out his insidious curse. His spell had been cast and its strength had not been as diminished as they had hoped; here was the evidence of the success of his evil doings. Den asked Churl to dip his feet back into the water. Churl was quick to remove his tired feet because as Den had inwardly predicted, the water was extremely cold. Not just the water, but the wind was cool and blowing directly from the north. Den, Fannie and Quay'Sea all understood that they needed to move more quickly than they had planned. The Society needed the information they carried so that a counter spell could be conjured to protect southern Adnil and even Shangie.

Fannie instilled the entire group, including the horses with vitality and stamina so that they could travel. They rode through the night and fuelled by Fannie's magic, they rode the entire following day. They stopped to sleep for a few hours to enhance Fannie's magic.

On the fourth day, the ragged group passed through the Northman Gates and headed directly for the palace. They were slowed to a walk inside the city and finally arrived at The Society's grounds at dusk.

CHAPTER 34

V WATCHED FROM INSIDE his bubble cocoon as his quarry made their getaway. He had underestimated the twins and now he faced a setback due to his own miscalculation. He raged at himself while he drained his power to sustain his own safe environment not only around himself but around his entire castle. The magic that he used to create his Enclave depended on the frozen ground especially around the foundation stone, engraved with all the power signatures, deep below the structure. If the stone thawed and cracked, the entire structure would likely collapse and deprive V of his precious children and all of his minions who would perish as it crumbled. He needed his children to carry on his legacy and he needed his followers to work his current plans.

V was further enraged that such a small defenceless girl could have fooled him into educating her so that she could use those practiced gifts against him. He would investigate how this had happened and those who were responsible would pay dearly for their transgression.

V grew gradually weaker as the time passed. His fury helped him as he held himself and his castle together for 2 full days before he was able to cause the cold to permeate Den's enchantment enough to relax his effort. The heat which Den had conjured had caused all the ice and snow within sight of the castle to thaw and melt away. The Enclave was a crusty granite bastion which stood on a barren coastline of boulders covered with a salty white residue. Soon enough the snow would return but the desolate rocky landscape was a constant sore reminder of how V had been defeated in his own stronghold. Just looking at the arid terrain enraged V to the point of distraction. He had depleted his power thus he was unable to react to the indignity immediately; he needed to rest and regain his strength and his perspective before he could devise an exclusive plan concocted specifically to deal with the infuriating twins.

V's followers rallied to his aid once he re-entered his Enclave. He linked with each individual member and candidate separately and siphoned some of their power to replenish his diminished supply. During his link with Bardook, he perused the memories of Fannie's education. This was his only opportunity to touch a small part of Fannie's mind since that untalented Mushookoalah had fled with his friends. V was anxious to dole out consequences to that corpulent clod and to his spindly conspirator as well.

Since Moira had not been seen since the battle on the snow, the membership assumed that she had died, giving her life to protect or assist her master. V had forbidden anyone from climbing up to the high tower so Moira's effigy would not be discovered anytime soon. Molisana took the opportunity of Moira's absence to ingratiate herself with V, hoping to replace Moira as V's favoured concubine. She dressed provocatively when she was summoned to V's chambers even though she would feel the iciness of his chambers in the silken folds of her scanty garb. He was planning to tap her energy reserves to help quench his thirst for power. She was pleasing to the eye and she did not seem even remotely phased by his scarred visage. V linked with her mind and was pleased with the destructive merits he found there. She had linked with many of the members at the Enclave and V laughed out loud when he determined how she had cheated to gain her treasured chess championship. As he siphoned her energy he searched her mind and was intrigued to see that she had linked with Mushookoalah. The dominoes fell into place in V's mind; it was Molisana's arrogance that V had read in Mushookoalah's mind when he was searching for a grain of evil left there by Fannie. There was no evil in the twin that he had nurtured and educated under the false assumption that he would eventually be able to turn her toward the dark arts. Exasperation caused V to violently tear himself from Molisana's mind. She would remain unconscious for days but V was beyond caring. This wisp of talented arrogance had caused him to be misled and she would face the consequences of her unknowing folly. V left her on the frozen floor of his chamber where she had collapsed in her inappropriate garments. If she survived his harsh exit from her mind and managed to keep from freezing to death, she would beg for death when V later toyed with her mind and her body.

V stormed out of his chamber, slamming the doors and magically sealing them so that Molisana could suffer her icy privacy. He composed himself and glided down the stairs where he sounded the chimes which called for an assembly of all of his followers in the main hall of the Enclave. With a grim expression, V stood in his place of power, before the statue of Manfred, as his minions arrived and stood quietly, awaiting their master's address. He wore a long black cloak with a cowelled hood and sleeves. From a deep pocket he pulled a pouch which contained small shards of granite, much like the rock from which the castle was composed. One hundred and eleven minions stood in rapt attention as V explained that the day had arrived for them to go forth and begin to take their deserved control of this northern continent. The congregation was inspired and anxious to use the gifts that they had honed and enhanced with their master's guidance. V announced that this was graduation day and hence all of the 111 were considered members. Bardook would co ordinate their assignments but V had a special gift for each one of them that would enable them to communicate with him no matter what distance they travelled to do their duty. The members fell into line and came forward one at a time to receive their gift from their revered master. Bardook was first; he stepped up to V and extended his right hand. V held Bardook's hand and jabbed a shard of granite into Bardook's middle finger in the place where he would wear a ring. V spoke an ancient word of binding which caused the shard to encircle Bardook's finger and attach itself to the fine bone of his finger. From this moment, Bardook would always be a part of this castle and a part of V himself. V sealed the bargain by forming a mind link with his loyal follower to firmly entrench himself into his mind. Once healed into place, the granite ring could not be removed and would act as a communication device to allow a mind link between servant and master. Bardook prostrated himself on the floor before his master and pledged his allegiance to the cause. V stood aloof and beckoned for the next member to approach. It took hours to brand all of the members with their own granite rings. No one was wasted or rejected at this ceremony. V understood that he would need all the minions he could muster to accomplish the mission he had initiated. Even the old individuals who had managed to survive their harrowing journeys north were appointed as members and subjected to the ceremony.

 It was an old hag who approached V that caused him to fume inwardly at his own lack of initiative with the candidates as they arrived at his Enclave. He had been preoccupied with his scheming and Moira and now he was once again reminded that his lack of attention to detail could lead to his undoing. When he linked with the decrepit female, to complete her passage into his inner circle and to ensure his ability for future communion, he learned what this hag had been trying to disclose since her arrival at the castle. No one had paid her any attention because they believed that she would soon become one of the weak un-chosen who would find herself abandoned to the elements. Now, too late, V was finally aware of why Fannie and Den were so important. Manfred had been adamant that they search out twins to add to their arsenal of power but now the reason was clear; Manfred had been searching specifically for Den and Fannie.

This crone was a friend of an old midwife's assistant who had related a story of a set of twins who had been spirited away from their rightful parents to be raised on the southern continent. They showed signs of being gifted; they had the eyes that he had looked upon during a battle not so long ago. Losing a set of powerful twins was disheartening and infuriating but losing the twins who were a part of the royal family of Adnil was unforgivable. V had only himself to blame and he cursed his own lack of involvement with the candidates.

With the ceremonies complete, V dismissed the throng to eat and sleep so that they could prepare for their departures which were scheduled to take place over the next several weeks.

V and Bardook retired to a private chamber where V provided specific information regarding the first steps of his planned domination. Bardook scribed lists of member's names and their assignments so that he could manage the travel plans. The membership would spread themselves throughout the populated areas of Adnil and begin appropriating land, power and dominion for their master.

V bid Bardook to follow him to his secret library where he kept his collection of appropriated scrolls and ancient books that would enable them to use the dark arts from this remote location. It was in a scroll carried here by a junior member that V had learned how to cast the spell he had conjured on the tower. All of the signatures and glyphs that would be required to amplify power were sketched and explained in the texts that other members had added to V's collection. This library was V's real treasure; with all the information he had gathered, he would certainly never be defeated again.

Bardook followed V down into the bowels of the castle. Before V turned into the labyrinth which protected his library, he warned Bardook not to lose sight of him or he could remain lost and wander listlessly till he collapsed and froze to death in the complex maze. Minutes later, the pair came upon the remains of a perfectly frozen and preserved Carl. He had apparently escaped the wall where Den had incapacitated him only to become lost in his master's labyrinth. This grizzly find only caused V to pause and guffaw as he continued on his way with Bardook in close pursuit. Bardook was clearly more affected by Carl's fate; he had been a good friend before he was sent to infiltrate The Society. The demise of Carl was certainly the loss of a loyal member and of a precious magical resource. Bardook hurried along behind V and in less time than he estimated it would take to eat his evening meal, they arrived at the centre of the maze and he was dumbfounded by the immense library hidden there.

V could see that Bardook was amazed and this was good because this room would soon become Bardook's new home. His apprentice had the power to conjure food and drink and he would be able to make himself comfortable in this protected chamber deep below the fortress that was the Enclave. V explained that Bardook was to eventually remain in this chamber, once all of the membership had been sent on their way, not only to guard the precious writings but to read and learn all that he could. V would come to him and this would be the control centre from which they would co-ordinate their assault on Adnil. Bardook showed a moment of concern at the thought of being imprisoned in a chamber, protected by a labyrinth, from which he could never exit on his own but his trust in his master was absolute so like a loyal clan member, he accepted this new proviso.

V glided over to one of the crowded shelves and retrieved an old scroll. As he turned back toward Bardook he paused and fingered the scroll while concentrating with his tactile awareness. Someone had recently touched this parchment; there was a ghost of someone's presence attached to the fibres that he stroked with his fingers. Fannie's spirit was certainly apparent; V expected as much because he had given Bardook permission to allow Fannie to read the texts that V himself had personally retrieved and made available. There was another fleeting presence that V was having difficulty identifying. It was Shilinar B'Edard. V cursed himself for not disposing of those meddling boys. If Fannie had not taken them as her friends, they would have been frozen in the barren wasteland long ago. Instead, the interfering pair had managed to fool him and now somehow invade his privacy. How had that spindly peon managed to solve the labyrinth and gain access to these precious secrets? Bardook saw V's mood change and he backed away to give his master plenty of room. He had seen what could happen when V had nowhere to aim his fury. Having regained mental control, V spun on his heel and made for the exit. Bardook trotted to keep up with his master lest he become lost in these complex passageways.

CHAPTER 35

THE SUN HAD fully set on the horizon of the Western Sea as the group of eight made their way through the gate that led to the complex populated by The Society. They had been unable to send word of their imminent arrival so they caused quite a stir as they rode their exhausted horses across the common toward the rear stables. The news of their arrival spread quickly and soon Morgan himself, along with many of the membership, was rushing across the yard to greet the entourage. The chancellor was so elated to see them all safely returned; he neglected to directly scold Den about his surreptitiously leaving the grounds without permission to engage in a personal conquest to find Fannie. Morgan's suspicions about Carl were confirmed when he noted the boy's obvious absence.

Food would be served and damp towels provided but the group would have to wait for the respite they so sorely needed. Morgan wanted a full account of everything that had taken place since he had lost touch with the search party after they had left the crossroads. Long embraces and good wishes were exchanged as they all made their way across the grounds toward Morgan's quarters. The large group which had gathered around the returning campaigners was instructed to remain in the portico and only Archel was invited to join the group for the private debriefing.

Archel had served as Morgan's right hand while Quay'Sea had led the search party into the north. She had proven herself to be more than competent and confident with her personal gifts and her considerable powers. She consistently exhibited the virtues that The Society was based upon. Morgan's respect and reliance on the young member had grown significantly stronger during this time of turmoil.

Each affiliate of the group of eight had their own story to tell. After Fannie was formally introduced and officially invited to join the membership of The Society, the intimate party munched on the refreshments and listened aptly as they all took their turns to retell their personal memories of their ordeals.

Den spoke about his trip to The Port of Merle with Carl and how they had gained passage on a fisher's barge to make their way north. It was only when they spied the castle Enclave that Den knew with a certainty that his sister was a captive in that gruesome edifice. Very soon, Den learned that Carl had betrayed him and was actually leading him into a trap where he could also be taken prisoner by the lord of the castle. It was a stroke of fate that the two had entered the castle through a passageway that led into the dark underground where Carl was unable to use his gift to battle Den. Without fire, Carl had been helpless when Den had frozen him to the icy stone walls in the bowels of the Enclave. Den was not aware of Carl's lot but he was sure that he had not laid eyes on him since he left him adhered to the cold wall.

Den described the castle and how it appeared to be designed in a magical way, constructed entirely of grey granite. As he depicted the structure, Fannie nodded her concurrence; she added a few details, focusing on the strange statues that adorned the main hall and the top of the highest tower. Morgan's thoughtful expression turned grim and he explained that from what Fannie portrayed, he believed these statues were more than they appeared. They may well be encapsulating living beings trapped inside a frozen image of themselves. His concern and compassion were apparent as he wiped a tear from his plump cheek before he bade Den to continue.

Den gave a full account of his meeting with Shilinar B'Edard in the lower reaches of the castle and how, without the boy's help, he may have become lost beyond discovery. With heartfelt emotion, he recounted his reunion with his precious twin sister while surrounded by Enclave members and candidates. Den told how Shilly and Mushy facilitated his concealment in Fannie's chamber, while a plan could be formulated to evade the Enclave without informing Shilly and Mushy about their actual motives. Vigour was a powerful telepath and he would certainly have stripped the information from the boys' minds. Shilly interrupted to enlighten Den that he did, in fact, suspect that an escape was planned and he was very appreciative to have been included along with Mushy. Fate had interceded once again; V did not think the boys were important enough to bother scanning them on an ongoing basis or he would certainly have been ready to stop them.

Den praised the boys for their bravery when the four had run across the barren ice to attempt to reach the dinghy behind the huge boulder. V had paralysed them with pain which caused Den and Fannie to turn and face V in a magical battle. Den meticulously explained each step of the battle, clarifying each spell he had cast and how V had retaliated. Den dwelled for some time recounting the spell that they interrupted by escaping at that particular time. The rings of vibrating sound and the blue liquid were of special interest to Morgan. Fannie's short mind link with V had explained that the spell he had cast was aimed at changing the weather patterns of the northern continent. It was going to become cold and The Society needed to immediately determine a way to curb or defuse the magic that was already gaining a stronghold and doing its damage. Den mentioned seeing the blue flashes in the water which Churl and Bin had discovered on their return journey through Kandar. The magic was moving quickly; the menacing blue flickers had turned the water cold and the concern which this had raised caused the group of eight to speed their return, aided by magic. Morgan was wringing his hands whilst taking in all the information and cataloguing it in his logical mind. Who was this Vigour and why was his target the climate of the entire continent?

Quay'Sea took over the retelling from the time he had joined the foursome on the barren beachhead. He digressed to explain how his search party had taken the northern fork at the crossroads which had led them to Ben's Inn at The Bay of Glaciers. Carlotta mentioned a package which was still in her possession; Ben had asked her to seek out his daughter Lily who apparently lived at the North Point Enclave. There had been no opportunity to seek out Lily so the sealed package was still in her deep pocket. She handed the small parcel to Morgan who would study its contents later. Quays continued his dialogue; he expounded the coincidental and auspicious appearance of the fishers who saved them from a long and arduous trek by dogsled to reach North Point. Without the passage by sea, they would have been late arriving at North Point and the escape may well have been thwarted. Morgan considered the coins paid to the fishers as well spent and nodded his agreement.

Their voyage by sea from North Point to The Port of Merle had been uneventful except for the rest and communion the group had the opportunity to share. Quay'Sea concluded by affirming that he also held a deep concern regarding the blue flashes in the water that his group had seen in the creek in Kandar.

Churl, Bin and Mushy had nothing to add but Shilly was quite sure that Morgan would be more than fascinated with the information he could provide. Shilly was a modest young man by nature, so it was awkward for him to expound his gifts and abilities in the company of this talented group. They all listened patiently, even though they were all badly in need of sleep. Shilly explained that he was an accomplished artist and he had the ability to recall any symbol, written work or artistic rendering that he had seen and he could also solve any puzzle or riddle that was posed. Before he had been lured to the northern Enclave, he had made his living entertaining the townsfolk with his abilities of recall and riddle unravelling. Because he was not chosen to be tutored and have his gifts nurtured at the Enclave, he became bored and explored the castle to a greater extent than the others in this room. Especially during the time when Mushy had been incapacitated with his mysterious illness, Shilly had spent considerable time in the lower levels of the castle. He described how he found a labyrinth that was very difficult to solve but once he recognised the pattern he solved the clever maze quickly. Overcoming the labyrinth was secondary to what he found at the centre. The library he had stumbled upon was filled with writings, ancient texts, scrolls, parchments and tablets. On his first visit, and several visits thereafter, Shilly did not realize that this was a forbidden area. Because it was unguarded he had wrongly assumed that he was free to borrow the items and read them if he wished. He had absorbed the information in a multitude of books and scrolls before he realized that these were obviously precious belongings and he was doubtlessly unwelcome. Thereafter he was cautious when he exchanged his reading material so as not to be seen. Den was the first person to have seen Shilly anywhere near the library. Morgan was engrossed as Shilly rattled on. The young artist informed Morgan and the others that he would be delighted to begin recreating the writings in their entirety if it would be of use to The Society. The chancellor was beside himself with enthusiasm and he assured Shilly that this may well be the edge they needed to overcome the disaster that was on its way. Fannie suggested a 3-way mind link with herself, Den and Shilly to help sift through the information he kept safely etched in his memory and to choose the specific data that was most relevant to defeating the spell that was currently threatening the climate of Adnil. All agreed that this was the most logical course of action. Almost asleep on their feet, the group of eight was dismissed to get the rest their bodies required before anything useful could be accomplished.

CHAPTER 36

MORGAN SAT SOLEMNLY concentrating in his private garden as the sun broke over the rooftops of Manek. Quay'Sea would soon join him and they would be heading over to the castle to respond to the summons of Queen Zelebeth. She had been kept privy to the events that had been occurring but she did not yet understand the gravity of the situation and what it might mean for her realm. Morgan himself had just learned all the details from Den, Fannie and Quay'Sea's group the previous evening. Other than Quays, all the others were still slumbering and regaining their strength after their long forced ride. The Queen and Prince Archer must be informed and made ready to prepare the northern continent for a siege by magic. Zelebeth had the allegiance of all her subjects and was well loved and admired but the human forces at her disposal were not necessarily the resources she would need to fight the battle that rapidly approached.

Morgan hated bringing bad news to the Queen; he had known her since she was born and he felt protective and fatherly towards her. She had played and spent time with all of the magicians and sorcerers within The Society's walls and now that she was matured and Queen, Morgan had a difficult time letting go of the little girl in his memory. Causing her worry and anguish were foreign to Morgan but he understood that she needed to know everything. Everything included being informed about the true identities of both Den and Fannie. Morgan had kept their identities closely guarded in an effort to maintain their safety but Zelebeth had a right to know that her realm had a prince and princess who could succeed her to the throne if the need ever arose. She had a brother and a sister to acquaint herself with. Before Den and Fannie could be told who they really were, Zelebeth and Archer needed to hear the truth from Morgan.

Quay'Sea entered the garden through the gardener's gate and walked briskly over to where Morgan was sitting, deep in thought. Without disturbing his mentor, he sat in the chair opposite Morgan and helped himself to the cheese and crisps on the low table. The chai was still hot so he poured himself a steaming cupful and waited to hear what Morgan had decided to do. He would offer his counsel only if Morgan requested it.

Rather than speak, Morgan rose from his chair and bade Quay'Sea follow him as he used the same gardener's gate where Quays had entered to lead him out to the edge of the common. He fell in stride with Morgan and they walked across the common which had little activity at this early hour. Today was the day, he told Quay'Sea, when we have to tell the Queen that she has twin siblings. Quay'Sea was relieved that the secret would finally be in the open and the twins could assume their rightful places as heirs to the throne of Adnil. The King had perished well before his time and had left his young daughter to rule but she had not yet produced an heir. A throne with no heir was precarious at best and with conflict on the horizon, Den and Fannie could provide the stability that was so dearly needed. The two men climbed the numerous stairs leading to the embellished entry way that would take them into the hall where they would wait for Zelebeth to call for them. Although she rarely engaged in such pomp and circumstance with Morgan, this was an official meeting that required solemnity.

Only moments after their arrival, Morgan and Quay'Sea were approached by a page who led them into the audience chamber at the top of a long marble staircase. The room was indescribably decorated and furnished with lavish chairs for the guests who were often entertained. Artfully carved and jewel encrusted double thrones sat on a pink marble dais which was slightly raised to keep the royal couple elevated and easily seen and heard. Several of the chairs were occupied by Zelebeth's advisors and councillors; everybody turned to greet Morgan and Quay'Sea as they were escorted into the audience chamber. Zelebeth imparted her special half smile at her fatherly magician. Rather than bow and seat themselves to begin their consultation, the two men approached the throne and Morgan begged pardon but he had need of the royal couple's ears for a private matter that could be shared with the present company at a later time if Zelebeth deemed it necessary. Archer was caught off guard but Zelebeth elegantly rose from her throne and bid her entourage retire for the present. Her shimmering golden over-garment swept the floor behind her as she descended the dais to embrace her fatherly mentor affectionately. Archer followed his Queen's example and joined her in the seating area where he welcomed Morgan and Quay'Sea in a less formal manner. The foursome sat facing each other and Zelebeth's curiosity was palpable.

Morgan did not keep her in suspense for more than a moment. He assured her that he would provide her with all the information gathered in the north directly but first he had something to impart that required this requested privacy. Without appearing to behave in an untoward manner, Morgan divulged the secret he had guarded for a very long time.

The Queen sat dumbfounded as her Prince held her fragile hand and tried to take in the news himself. The emotions Zelebeth experienced ranged from surprise to disgust, to compassion and to anxiety. She was disgusted by her own Queen Mother's capacity for coldness and hatred; she was full of compassion for the twins who had managed to survive against all odds. Most of all, Zelebeth was very eager to meet her estranged brother and sister. She wanted to be the one to tell Den and Fannie that they were her long lost and unheard of siblings. That reunion would have to wait till later in the day because the chancellor of The Society had other serious matters, to discuss with the royal couple, which could not wait.

Zelebeth and Archer were dismayed and concerned about the report delivered by Morgan and Quay'Sea. The Queen deferred all magical matters to her trusted friend and mentor. She was confident that The Society could find a way to protect her citizens from the malevolence that currently lurked in the north, threatening to foul her peaceful land and its populace. She had the wherewithal to muster armies if the need arose but she was wise enough to accept that an army would stand little chance of defeating the evil that threatened her land. Her faith lay with the gifted individuals whom her father had welcomed to the palace so many years ago. Fate had brought Morgan and old King Gaylord together to share a friendship and a bond that made this day possible. Zelebeth had The Society which would fight to keep her realm safe and undamaged. She bid Morgan to return that evening with her siblings to share refreshments with the Queen and her Prince. She asked Morgan to keep her apprised of any developments regarding the "Northern Threat". She had kept them away from his labours too long already, so she gave Morgan and Quay'Sea leave to return to their work.

The men busied themselves with planning and organization schedules till midday when the newly refreshed group joined them to receive their assignments. Den and Fannie were very concerned about their farm family and they requested leave to visit Jok, El and the children. Morgan was reticent to divulge too much information before the meeting with the Queen so he suggested that Bin and Churl fetch the family to stay at The Society's guest houses for a time. He assured Den and Fannie that their skills were needed and a leave was out of the question for the time being. Morgan was also secretly concerned that Vigour might take out his anger on the defenceless family. Surly V was aware of the location of the farm where Fannie had been abducted by Jeeree and his thugs and he was liable to aim his rage at Fannie's loved ones now that he had lost her.

Bin and Churl were dispatched that very afternoon and they were pleased to be the bearers of the good news of Den and Fannie's return. They were confident that they could convince the family to join them for an extended stay at The Society compound, especially when Jok considered his family's safety. They departed in a large wagon and promised to return with Jok, El and the children as soon as possible.

Den and Fannie were informed that they were summoned by Queen Zelebeth to appear for a private audience that evening. Morgan and Quay'Sea would be joining the twins for their meeting at the palace after the evening meal. The afternoon was spent setting up a chamber with all the necessary accoutrements necessary for Shilinar to begin recreating the secrets he had memorized in V's library. The paraphernalia included parchment paper, copper plates with etching solutions, inks of every colour, pens, paintbrushes, clay and sculpting tools. Mushy worked alongside his best friend to help keep him supplied as his needs arose. As Mushy made the chamber ready, Shilly sat locked in a mind link with both Fannie and Den going over all the information he had catalogued in his ordered mind. They methodically studied each text, scroll, glyph and signature to better choose where Shilly should begin his recreations. They located and focused on the spell they believed V had cast from the tower but they had no way of ascertaining exactly which signatures Moira had created to enhance, shape or boost V's casting. Shilly had a starting point and his work would keep him occupied for a long time. Mushy was Shilinar's constant companion and often appeared at the chamber door with food for Shilly and himself. Mushy organized the librarians who were charged with cataloguing the writings which Shilly produced. The work was slow and often arduous but the boys persevered and continued to work to the best of their abilities. They would eat and sleep in their private area so that Shilly could provide as much information as possible as quickly as possible.

Den and Fannie made their way over to the mess where they joined Quay'Sea for the evening meal. They were quite excited to meet the Queen and her Prince and they wondered why they were being accorded the privilege of a private audience. Quays assured them that all would be revealed in good time. Well sated, the threesome made their way to one of the many fountains in the common where Morgan already waited. He wore his official robes of office and the twins were impressed and suddenly anxious about this audience. They followed Morgan through the gardens and up the imposing marble stairs. Inside, the four visitors were shown to a room that could be considered quaint compared to the opulent main audience chamber. This smaller area was furnished with comfortable chairs and small wooden tables that were inlaid with silver and gold designs. Fresh flowers scented the room and added their beauty to the calming ambience. Morgan showed them to their seats and they only waited a few moments before the Prince and his Queen entered the room. They all stood and bowed deeply before the handsome royal couple. The tall, handsome Prince towered over his beautiful and fragile Queen. She locked eyes with Fannie once the twins regained their normal postures. Fannie sucked in her breath and held it as she studied Zelebeth's features. This Queen looked so much like her very own brother; the violet eyes, the long raven curls that were so elegantly coiffed. Zelebeth invited them to seat themselves comfortably because she had a story to tell.

Both Fannie and Den sat engrossed in the tale spun by the young Queen. She retold the story just as she had heard it that very afternoon from Morgan. Zelebeth explained that she had learned this true story from a trusted friend and she believed it with all her heart, especially now that she had met her twin siblings. The late Queen D'Enfanel had acted immorally when she sent her babes to be destroyed. Her fear and suspicion of anything magic had led her to behave wickedly and she had paid with her life when she refused the potions and spells that would have saved her life when she became dreadfully ill. D'Enfanel had lied to her husband and provided him with the corpse of a child who had died that afternoon in the slums of Manek and she believed that she took that secret with her to her grave. Fate had been with the twins and guided the midwife's assistant to flee with the infants and place them in a far off land where they could live and grow to become the individuals who sat here today. Their very names were proof of their lineage; D'Enfanel had been divided into Den and Fannie.

D'Enfanel had been right about one thing, the twins were gifted and powerful users of magic. In the morning, Morgan had explained to the Queen that Den and Fannie were sorely needed at The Society. Zelebeth acknowledged Den and Fannie's gifts and extolled her appreciation for their efforts to help protect the citizens of Adnil. She wanted to spend time with them each day but she knew that their work would keep their visits brief. Zelebeth would be satisfied knowing that they were close by and safe. The hour was late and the audience which had become a family reunion was at an end. Zelebeth stopped the twins when they moved to bow and told them that they would never be required to bow to her; they were a part of the royal family.

This had been a very exciting two days for Fannie and Den. They needed some time together to re-examine all that they had learned. Den linked with Fannie and smirked as he asked his newly appointed princess to come and sit by the fountain for a short time. They agreed that it would take some time to assimilate all the news they had received and the repercussions of their new statures had yet to be revealed. They were looking forward to seeing Jok and El. The children would have grown and they would surely enjoy The Society's hospitality and the palace's gardens and beach. Before they decided to retire for the night, they vowed to face each day as it came and use their gifts to help The Society in any way possible.

CHAPTER 37

BARDOOK WAS RUN off his feet during the hectic preparations at the Enclave. He sent 55 pairs of members to the areas they were assigned throughout the northern continent. They were dispatched to Lochko, Messo, The Port of Merle, The Fork, Zoloto, Oozo and even Manek itself. Many others were sent to less populated areas in the Prain Territory and Kandar but their missions were no less important. They were V's ambassadors who would inform the citizens that their new Regent was Vigour. Anyone who did not choose to pay him homage would suffer greatly. Most of the travelling members would reach their destinations by the turn of the season but some members would not reach their remote destinations till well into the spring. If V's spell was taking hold, spring would be late . . . very late. The individuals of the membership were instructed to warn the people of what was to come and to lay the blame on The Society. V's ambassadors were to infer that the Queen's sorcerers had gone awry and caused a freeze which threatened to starve the northern continent. Lay people, especially those who lived in remote areas, were prone to superstition and were often leery of anything magic. V's minions were warned not to use magic publicly to enhance their likelihood of being accepted and trusted by the people. The population would surely turn to Vigour to save their crops and feed their families. The plan was insidious and Bardook had to admire V's firm resolve and his deviousness.

Bardook was very tired of being cold and the thought of causing everything to become even colder gave him a shiver deep in his soul. It would not do to question or even think of doubting his master. The ring he wore, attached to his very being, allowed V to enter and search his mind at will. V could reach the mind of each and every member, no matter how far they travelled. He could visit their minds and provide new instructions when needed. Fortunately, V could only visit one member at a time so he did not dwell in one mind very long. The ring ensconced in each member's finger gave a tingling and icy warning when their master was making his connection. V kept a strict account of each member's headway and met with Bardook in the library each evening.

Bardook was doing his best to document the spells that V would need to ultimately defeat the magicians at The Society when the fateful day eventually arrived. V intended to freeze the continent so that he could comfortably make the journey to Manek where he would face his adversaries personally.

The 2 sets of twins were V's next priority. Lily had adorned the tower for more than a year and the twins were accustomed to their surrogate mothers. The boys were older and displaying their gifts when the need caused the necessity. They were able to move objects and cause general mayhem for their personal amusement. The girls were more timid when displaying their powers but V knew that they were mind linked, content to keep their gifts confined for the most part. Kern and Zephyr would stay at the Enclave and Bardook would soon take over their education and nurture them in the dark arts. Shandra and Frosh needed a more secret location to grow and mature before V deemed them ready for preparation to meet their destinies. He would personally travel to The Bay of Glaciers where he would inform Big Ben of his daughter's illness which had led to her sad demise. The twins could be left with their grandparents who would shelter and care for them until V wanted them back.

V was vain enough to want his face to once again appear handsome and unscarred. His magic amulet had been torn from his neck by the winds during the battle on the tower. Before he travelled to The Bay of Glaciers, he intended to have his scars disguised. V cast a finding spell to cause his lost necklace to shine and vibrate. That evening, in the darkness, V scoured the rocky surfaces around the Enclave until he retrieved his amber glyph. Moira had possessed quite a talent; pity she had not been loyal enough to stand with V when the battle raged. He fitted the amber creation with a secure clasp and hung it around his neck on a chain made of silver and enchanted granite. He did not plan to lose this amulet again. Adnil needed a fetching regent.

The Enclave was still populated by many servants, some of whom were detailed to prepare the travelling arrangements to The Bay of Glaciers. The huge snow dogs were harnessed to a lightweight sleigh in which V, his daughters and their servant could sit comfortably. The servant held the girls snugly under a fur swathe where the cold could not reach them. V sat, lightly dressed, on a seat from which he could control and steer the dogs. V infused the dogs with magical energy which would allow them to run from

North Point to The Bluff without rest. The trip from North Point to The Bay of Glaciers should take no more than a few days. V remembered how he and Moira had struggled their way to North Point on their first expedition to build the castle. With all of Manfred's teachings and his library full of information, V was now much smarter and considerably stronger.

Ben's inn looked just as it did when Vigour had last seen it. The warmth inside would be insufferable for V but he did not intend to stay for very long. Ben and Helga were distraught when they were informed of the news of Lily's demise. V did his very best to present himself as the inconsolable husband and he elicited pity and compassion from Lily's grieving parents. Both Ben and Helga were saddened but delighted to take over the care of their sweet twin granddaughters. Shandra and Frosh would have a place to grow and mature incommunicado.

Vigour explained that he would be extremely occupied, for the foreseeable future, studying ways in which he could help deter the magic which had been set free in the south. He admitted that he was gifted and felt it was his duty to help his fellow citizens. V described how he had learned that the Queen's magicians had unleashed a magic that would cause the entire continent to freeze and eventually starve, due to lack of food. V had collected books and scrolls which may hold the information needed to defy the magic of the evil southern sorcerers. V implored Ben and Helga to pass this information to any travellers who passed through The Bay of Glaciers. The populace deserved to know and understand what was happening to them and who was ultimately responsible for their suffering. The royals and the magicians of The Society in Manek must be held accountable for the destructive force they had unleashed on the continent of Adnil. Ben had always believed that Vigour was a good man but now he admired his courage and fortitude. He solemnly promised to pass the information to all the people who lived in the area and he would be sure to inform travellers so that they too could carry the frightening news.

V did not rest for even a night at Ben's inn. The heat in the building was discomfort enough but the main reason for his lack of delay was his need to return and coordinate his departed members. They must be guided and monitored so they too could continue to spread the lie that V had professed. The propaganda must be proliferated to every village, town, city, travelling minstrel and entertainer. Each person, who was told the false story, would aid V's effect of spreading the news quickly and efficiently. The population must be made to turn against Zelebeth and her compassionate advisors to leave the citizens in need of a strong and powerful leader. V, the saviour, would be available to take his rightful place as King and ultimate ruler of Adnil and the people would accept and love him until it was too late for them to change their muddled minds.

CHAPTER 38

SOCIETY MEMBERS WHO were in the field gathering information, helping with the healing of illness and other things like crop infestations, were making their way back to the palace in Manek in great numbers. They all carried the same news; the people were angry and afraid of the sorcerers who were responsible for causing the cold which was invading the land to a greater degree each day. Some members returned with injuries that had been inflicted by irate farmers who were still waiting for the spring which was not yet making its appearance. V's spell was making its effects apparent and the membership had successfully spread the propaganda implicating The Society as the power responsible for the paranormal climate changes.

Zelebeth called for an assembly of all of her most trusted advisors and The Society elite. Den and Fannie were included as both Society members and the Prince and Princess of Adnil. Morgan addressed the gathering and informed them of the dire news coming in from all parts of the continent. A general unrest and dissatisfaction with the governors was increasing and even escalating to violence in some areas. Shilinar B'Edard was making some headway with his recreations of Vigour's texts but as yet a counter spell had not been discovered. The Society was in a position to send out the gifted to protect small areas from the cold but a major solution to the creeping winter was not yet available. Using powers to create small compartments of warmth, much like the small bubble of heat generated by Den in the far north, farms and orchards could be protected by dispatched members but The Society simply did not have the manpower to warm the continent. Morgan had assigned several scholarly members to scour the writings that Shilinar was producing as quickly as humanly possible. When a solution was eventually found, The Society would be ready to act but as of yet, there was nothing they had retrieved that would be of any benefit. Zelebeth's assembly determined three things; Shilinar B'Edard should be given any and all the resources he required to continue his recreations, volunteers should return to the countryside to help protect crops which would soon become very necessary to feed the multitudes, and the Royal family must be accorded protection from any misinformed and possibly militant citizens who may want to cause them harm.

Den and Fannie were in demand; Zelebeth wanted them kept close to the palace and Morgan wanted them to mind link with Shilly to help him pick and choose the texts that might be most important. What the twins wanted was to spend quality time with Jok, El and the children. By this time, it should have been mid-summer but spring was barely making its appearance on the northern continent; even the lands north of the Davor Peaks on the southern continent were being affected. The snows which capped the Borealis Mountains were collecting and moving down the slopes where the lakes and waterways which fed the continent were freezing. Animals were migrating south where they could find a temperate climate in which they could bear their young and find food. Domestic animals could no longer be fed because the grazing fields were still dormant and the stored supplies were growing dangerously low. The lack of fishing and hunting was affecting the human population and news of people moving their families south had begun to reach the palace. Prince Archer was disheartened when news from Locan, his home country, arrived at the palace. The people of Queenstown had literally overrun Kingsport and food supplies were running low. The messengers informed the Prince that they barely made it through The Divide which would be sealed with snow and ice by now. The continent had been literally divided by the ice and snow which blocked the only mountain pass. Because the east was no longer accessible, the royal couple would be cut off from any communication until this climate could be influenced by The Society's magic.

Within weeks, there was civil unrest in Manek. Food shortages and frosty weather combined to make the once content populace into an unpredictable throng. The people were only one step away from a panic which would inevitably lead to looting and violence. Morgan counselled Zelebeth to move her family and advisors to a more secure location. The palace had not been built to defend against attack because peace had reigned in Adnil for generations. The old palace on Solosk which had been maintained as a summer resort could provide the sanctuary necessary during this dangerous time. The island could be cut off and protected by a small flotilla to better ensure the protection of the royals and their entourage. The Society would move their base of operations to the island as well, to continue their studies and keep the hopes of defeating V alive.

Morgan's good friend, Cresterman, was the captain of his own ship and he was also the owner of several smaller ships used for trading cargo. Morgan had confided in his friend and Cresterman was eager to be of service to the royal family. He had outfitted his traders with some weaponry and offered to move the large numbers of people to the safety of Solosk. Zelebeth promised Cresterman compensation and offered him a posting of General in her new fleet. The people would be moved and the treasury would be relocated to Solosk until the threat was routed. The flight had to be kept secret to ensure a safe departure. The ships were loaded with goods and a human cargo, and the Queen and her Prince were the last to board the lead ship in the Royal armada.

Shilinar continued his scribing while in transit so that he did not waste a moment. He was exhausted but he could not rest without feeling a plaguing guilt. Fannie discovered Shilly collapsed on the floor of his tiny cabin when she entered carrying a light repast for the hardworking boy. She immediately linked with him to try to determine what had befallen poor Shilly. She sent him energy and restful thoughts. It occurred to Fannie that she and Den should have been fortifying Shilly's powers on an ongoing basis. Fannie also determined that she could help scribe the Signatures and Glyphs that were less complex. She summoned Den and the three remained linked until Shilly was well enough to go on with his work. Shilly could not send information to Fannie or Den but the twins could pluck words and images from Shilly's mind, especially when he was wide open to their probes. Working together, they would have recreated most of V's library by the time the armada reached Solosk.

The ships hugged the coast of Adnak and then Sonda until they reached the Cormer port of Janine. Here, they travelled The Passage which opened onto The Gulf of King's Wealth, which was a calm inland sea. Their sea journey to Solosk was almost complete. The Prince was relieved that the journey was close to its end because his Queen had suffered from the water's movements. She had become sickly and unable to hold the nourishment she ingested. Fannie shared Archer's concern and convinced Zelebeth to accept her healing magic. Fannie calmed Zelebeth's queasy abdominals and she also discovered something that even Zelebeth did not yet know. The heirs of Adnil were on their way; the Queen was to give birth to triplets, all boys. The good news spread to the entire armada and a celebration would be in order when they arrived on Solosk. Birthing triplets would tax the young Queen's frail body but she felt confident, having heard how Fannie and Den had assisted El with her difficult delivery. This was a good omen; three was a sacred number and with her siblings' assistance, Zelebeth was poised and determined to deliver three healthy and strong sons.

Morgan stood on the deck of the lead ship as they sailed east, into the rising sun, along the island coast toward Verde. The silhouette of the summer palace was imposing against the morning sky which was streaked with orange and violet. The structure itself was small compared to the palace at Manek but it would suit the needs of the royal family and their loyal followers. General Cresterman and his crews would be able to blockade the island while The Society worked their magic business. The docks were filled with people and Morgan took pause until he realized that the news of their arrival had reached Verde through people who had seen the ships sailing along the coast. The congregation on the docks was happy and celebrating the arrival of ships laden with supplies. Zelebeth would have to address the crowd and share the reason why she had arrived on Solosk. If the population of this island could be convinced to remain loyal to the crown, everybody's safety could be ensured.

After her heartfelt address which held back no secrets, Zelebeth and her entourage were welcomed by a troubled and anxious crowd. She had won them over and they all seemed to need her guidance and nurturing. The palace would once again be the home of the royal family of Adnil and the islanders would remain loyal to their young Queen.

CHAPTER 39

V WAS JUBILANT AS he stepped gingerly between the signatures on the floor of his Enclave tower. The information he had gleaned through his communications with his scattered followers was keeping his mood buoyant and exultant. The people of the continent were fuelling their own anger over their frosty situation and that anger was aimed directly at the royal family and their precious Society. The allegiance of these sheep-like people was shifting towards V because they believed that the rumours of his ability to rescue them from their plight were actually true. They would be sadly disappointed when and if they actually realized that there was no rescue. The spell he had loosed was not reversible.

Bardook was a lonely man, trapped in this library, where he never knew if it was day or night, with only two young boys for company. The twins were prone to terrorizing the exasperated sorcerer with their childish antics which tended towards causing disorder and general mayhem. They were both generously gifted but their immaturity made it difficult for Bardook to focus those gifts in a direction of his choosing. This situation was becoming intolerable and Bardook was very sure that this was not the future he had envisioned for himself when he pledged his loyalty to Vigour. He had to keep these thoughts well hidden and he had learned a thing of two from studying Fannie's mind barrier. He could bury these secret feelings and thoughts in a place where V was unlikely to venture if he chose to invade Bardook's mind.

He required a way to leave this library if the need ever arose so each time V visited, Bardook followed his master a short way into the labyrinth. Bardook made insignificant markings low on the walls of the labyrinth that only he would notice. Each visit by V enabled Bardook to map out a little more of the confining maze. He knew he was close to being able to solve the maze when he reached the area where Carl's body still lay prone and frozen on the floor. Bardook looked sadly upon his friend and understood that V possessed not a single shred of compassion. This could just as easily have been Bardook himself, lying dead and forgotten on the floor like a piece of garbage not even worthy of disposal. Serious doubts were manifesting themselves in Bardook's mind and he had to keep them completely veiled behind his personal barrier.

V entered the library and wore his exhilaration like a cloak. Bardook had been making some progress with Kern and Zephyr who were behaving in an acceptable manner for the meantime. V discussed the news from the membership and his prediction for the next step in his plan for domination. They would wait out the winter which promised to be stalwart and when the following spring never arrived, V would be ready to visit his new domain. The population would have to be notified that all of V's efforts to defeat The Society's evil magic had failed. The populace must be convinced to storm the capital and destroy those responsible for this malevolence. Adnil's citizens would voluntarily rid V of the royal family and those who were protected in the palace at Manek.

Following his session with V, as his master was on his way to retire for the night, Bardook mapped the final turns in the confounding labyrinth. V would likely sleep well into the morning so Bardook took this opportunity to leave his makeshift prison. He was very curious why V had made it forbidden for anyone to go up to the high tower. His first foray out of the confining library would be used to unravel this secret. Bardook silently and cautiously made his way up the steep, dark stairway that would lead him to the windy platform where Lily vigilantly pointed her fragile arm toward the southeast. Before he reached his intended destination, Bardook was horrified by his unexpected find. Moira was believed to have died during the battle fought against the twins and their allies. This effigy, caught in mid-scream and apparent terror, proved that V had been responsible for Moira's absence after the battle. If the talented and vital Moira could provoke such a severe consequence, Bardook wondered what his fate would be if he disappointed the unstable master he had pledged to serve. It was certainly time to re-evaluate his tenuous position in this northern place where Bardook suddenly felt foreign and trapped. Anything that might go awry with V's plans would certainly be blamed on Bardook; he was the only one left in the Enclave upon whom V could vent his displeasure. Until an opportunity presented itself, Bardook decided to tread very softly around the lord of the castle.

Bardook took every precaution to disguise his ability to leave his library confinement. He never ventured out of his assigned space unless absolutely necessary and then he took special care to be sure that V was sleeping or entirely occupied. Bardook visited his old quarters to retrieve his satchel which contained several magical stones which he had collected during his travels before he was called to serve V.

With the twin boys slumbering an enchanted sleep, Bardook reached into his satchel and withdrew a ruby stone which would allow him to change the words in the texts he studied. The stone removed or changed the wording in any type of scroll or book so that it would become nonsensical to anyone who tried to read it. Only the spell caster had the power to re-order the words into their original and meaningful order. Methodically, Bardook cast his muddling spell over all of the writings in the library. This was an indemnity against V's possible wrath; he would never hurt or dispose of Bardook with his precious library held hostage. Holding this power over the written texts in the library gave Bardook a sense of security, even though it may be false. Although Bardook's powers were considerable, he knew he had no chance of defeating or even deflecting V's wrath if it was suddenly aimed at him. Like Fannie before him, he needed to make a plan to escape this situation, but as of yet he had not a clue as to how to make it so.

CHAPTER 40

WITH ALL OF V's texts, scrolls and various writings transcribed, Morgan was distressed to inform the Queen that there was no answer or counter-spell found to work against V's curse. He had been hopeful that V had used a spell that had a counter, but apparently V had not foreseen a need to ever change that which he had instigated. Shilinar had re-created the exact spell from a small parchment which he had read but the spell itself was ruled by the caster and only by eliminating the caster could the spell be overturned. This was a setback that no one had anticipated. The only solution lay in travelling back to the far reaches of Afshen to face Vigour in his own stronghold. If he could not be defeated, all was lost and Adnil would remain forever frozen under V's control.

Zelebeth wept openly for the fate of her people. They had been lied to and made to turn against the only individuals left who had the means to try to save them. She bid The Society to do as it must to put things to right. Morgan felt her helplessness and vowed to do all that he could to resuscitate the dwindling continent back to its resplendent self.

After meeting with the advisors and General Cresterman, Morgan returned to the Queen with a plan of action that he hoped would meet with her satisfaction. They suggested rebuilding one of the General's smaller ships to withstand the ice flows and the bergs that they would encounter during their voyage. Volunteers would be called for who were skilled sailors and chose to make the voyage to North Point. A number of Society members with various gifts would be presented with the opportunity to join the venture but it was paramount to include Quay'Sea, Fannie and Den. Zelebeth was hesitant to give her permission to put the lives of her siblings in harms way but she was eventually convinced that the foray had little chance of success without the two most gifted magic users. Fannie and Den knew V's only weakness was his aversion to heat. During the battle, they had deflected enough of V's concentration to enable their precarious escape by putting his environment in jeopardy. During their upcoming voyage they would strive to create a technique to incapacitate V completely. His ultimate destruction was the only way to save the entire continent.

Zelebeth worried for her unborn sons. She privately met with Fannie and beseeched her to return before the birthing time arrived. Zelebeth was convinced that her sons would never see this world without the intervention of her talented sister. Fannie assured the Queen that there were many talented members in The Society who would remain on Solosk and they were more than gifted enough to ease her delivery. Zelebeth was adamant that Fannie give her a solemn promise to return for the birth because she trusted no one else with the safety of the royal heirs. With promises in place, Fannie made her way to her chamber where she proceeded to pack several warm garments that would be essential during the voyage and certainly at North Point.

It had taken several days to load the ship with all the vital cargo that was deemed necessary. Morgan stood at the end of the pier and supervised as the last consignment was stored in the hold of the small but sturdy vessel. Everybody else was already on board waiting for Den and Fannie to arrive.

The twins were saying goodbye to Jok and El and persuading them that all would be well in short order. They tried to make the risk they were facing seem less dire in an attempt to prevent Jok and El from worrying. El missed Fannie terribly when they were parted because she was the only person with whom El could converse. Fannie told El to take care of her family and busy herself with commonplace chores to make the time apart fly by. She hugged El fiercely and told her she was expecting a huge apple cobbler upon her return to celebrate their victory. The children promised to help with the cobbler and Fannie and Den left the little family not really knowing if they would ever see them again.

The ship, which they re-named Fortune, set sail with Fannie and Den leaning on the gunwale and waving at Morgan who stood in the noon day sun, surrounded by members on the end of the empty pier. He wanted nothing more than to be with the band that was sailing off to attempt to save the north. Logic prevented Morgan from using his authority to place himself among the brave crusaders. He understood that if they failed in their task, he would be the only one left to guide what was left of The Society, here on Solosk.

General Cresterman was reticent to estimate their arrival at North Point because he was unsure about the conditions at sea. The climate change may have altered some of the currents and the water conditions since he had last travelled in that direction. He assured the members that they had many days at sea, ample time to formulate a plan of action for when they finally reached North Point. Challenging V in his own stronghold was a bold action that would probably be unexpected; if they caught V off guard, their likelihood of success would be substantially improved. Fannie and Den linked with every one of the members to give them a layout of the Enclave. They had decided on the point of entry that would give them a tactical advantage. The group would split up once they landed on the beach and Fannie would lead one group into the entrance that she had come through when she had first arrived by dogsled. Den would lead the second unit through the catacombs where he knew the secret entrance near the library, where he had first acquainted himself with Shilinar B'Edard. The membership practiced every spell they knew that could generate heat or fire. The Enclave boasted little that would burn so they concentrated on the production of magical heat. The members who were chosen to go on this critical mission were selected because their gifts included dominion over fire and other earth elements. From all that he had gathered, these were the powers that Morgan thought would best serve to defeat Vigour.

Everyone knew their spells and wore their personal amulets to amplify their powers. They were as ready as they could ever be to face this powerful adversary.

The General expertly steered the Fortune through treacherous seas and by mammoth icebergs. Once they passed onto the Northern Sea, the weather had proven more bitter than he had anticipated but the members had handily melted the ice which continuously formed around the rudder and made steering difficult. The sails were fortified with magical strength so that they would not crack and splinter apart under the icy build up. Without the gifted passengers, the General's ship would have been lost to the punishing Northern Sea. They were less than a day away from their destination and a snowstorm was conjured to disguise their surreptitious arrival. Surprise was paramount if their invasion of the Enclave was to succeed.

In the midst of blowing snow and zero visibility, two sizable dinghies were lowered into the sea as close to the shore as Cresterman could safely manoeuvre his sturdy ship. He lost sight of the dinghies almost as soon as they were loosed in the choppy sea. He recited a silent entreaty yearning for fate to smile on these brave crusaders. With only a handful of gifted members left onboard to protect his vessel from freezing, Cresterman dropped anchor to wait and see if he would welcome any victorious returning passengers to transport back toward the south or if his ship would come under attack and sink into this icy graveyard called the Northern Sea.

CHAPTER 41

V WAS THRILLED WITH the weather; snow and ice were the things he loved best. He sat in his icy chamber in a granite chair facing the frozen corpse of Molisana who still appeared provocative and inviting in her preserved state. Leaving her body for his constant perusal comforted V by reminding him of just how powerful he was. Pity she had not lasted long enough for him to inflict the pain she had deserved as a consequence for her gaffe. Still he was able to satisfy his arrogance each time he looked at Lily, Moira and now Molisana. They all served a purpose, two alive and trapped and Molisana dead and frozen.

It was time to communicate with his members. V clenched his fist and rested his forehead against his own stone ring and established contact with one of his many followers stationed in Manek. It seemed that the royal family had fled to avoid being massacred by their own loyal subjects. V was unconcerned; he would locate them and send the hordes to dole out the punishment that the Queen and her family deserved. He was willing to be patient because he was assured that his victory would taste even sweeter after the long anticipation. The city of Manek was a war zone. Those who did not choose to make their way south had stayed to loot and destroy that which had taken years to build. Fires burned out of control and everything of value had been stolen or ruined. V planned to leave that once bustling city forsaken and deserted as an example for the citizens to remember what the Queen had left as her legacy. Pleased with the news, V continued contacting various members in other areas of the continent.

Den led his group of members into the catacombs under the castle. It was as he had remembered the last time he made his way through these dark and frozen tunnels with Carl. He reached the place where he had left Carl to his fate; he was nowhere to be found. Maybe Carl had managed to find his way to the welcoming oasis of his master's bosom. Den ignited his tiny illuminating flame and led his team deeper into the bowels of the stronghold where they would find the room which opened up into the hallways that would lead them to the centre of V's power.

Fannie's group made their way into the castle without incident because it was literally empty. Fannie expected to be challenged and to have to fight her way into the castle itself but now she was concerned about the lack of people. What had happened to all the candidates and members who made this place their home a short time ago? Fannie gathered her team before the statue of Manfred in the main hall of the Enclave. She laid both of her hands on the statue to test Morgan's theory about someone actually being alive and trapped inside this marble prison. He was correct, Fannie sensed a life force but it was malevolent and hateful. She drew her thoughts back into herself and decided to leave this wicked man trapped in a place he probably deserved. Fannie communicated her position to Den and explained that the castle was deserted. She was planning to take her group up to the tower where she wanted to search the mind of the woman she now knew to be a prisoner. Den warned Fannie to take care in her movements because he did not want her to face V alone.

Fannie guided her troop to the stairway and warned them that it would be steep and dark. Their assent was slow and laborious and when Fannie stumbled over Moira's terrifying form, she almost cried out. Den remained linked with Fannie and he was also appalled with Moira's fate. Each member made their way past Moira and finally exited the doorway onto the platform at the top of the castle. They were all mesmerized by the beauty and the longing exuded by the statue standing proudly on its dais. Fannie lightly touched the face of the statue and was immediately filled with the emotions of the spellbound woman. She was filled with love, sadness, disappointment, and faith that she would one day be rescued from this icy prison. Fannie did not have the magic to release this suffering woman but she knew that this was Lily. Morgan was holding a package for her back on the island of Solosk. Two of the members who accompanied Fannie combined their strength and caused the statue to float above its base. They concentrated to slowly move the bulky effigy over the edge of the tower where they slowly lowered her to the beach where they gently placed her by a large boulder. Fannie hoped that someone in Den's group might have the expertise to release Lily from her incarceration. Fannie warned her companions to be especially quiet as they made their way back toward the main hall because they had to once again pass close to V's chamber.

Den was emerging into the hallway near the labyrinth entrance with his group quietly following. He heard footfalls and raised his hand to warn his cohorts to remain still and quiet. Den chanced a peek around the roughly hewn corner and found himself face to face with Bardook who thought he had been caught outside of his library by V. Bardook's look of relief caused Den to pause in his casting of the spell he had ready for just such an occurrence. Bardook held out his hands and begged Den to have mercy and to rescue him from this life filled with fear and anxiety. Den wasn't sure how to react to this strange meeting. Bardook did appear to be genuine in his request but Den was suspicious of his intentions. He had appeared to have been hiding in the hallway and Fannie agreed, through her link, that Bardook seemed to be afraid and desperate. This was the opportunity that Bardook had been waiting for; Den and Fannie could help him to escape or at least die trying.

Bardook informed Den that V was currently in his chamber making contact with all of the minions who had been sent far and wide to spread the propaganda implicating The Society as the magical users responsible for the climate change. He might be finished at any time or he may continue communing into the night. He told Den how he left V's gifted twin boys in the library where Bardook himself had been held captive until he found his way through the labyrinth. Den had studied the map of the labyrinth provided by Shilly so he knew how to enter and exit without following Bardook's subtle markings. Fannie voiced her concern that the children could not be left to stay in the library because if they should succeed in defeating Vigour, the castle would surely crush the children to death, if it collapsed as Den intended. Bardook entered the library, with Den, where he enhanced the enchantment which had kept the children asleep while Bardook did his wandering. Two of the members, Lucious and Kane, were assigned to bundle up and take the children to the beach and to find shelter behind the large boulder at the coastline and wait for the outcome of the ensuing confrontation with V. Lucious was skilled enough to create a heated bubble where he and Kane could wait comfortably with the children.

Bardook showed Den and Quay' Sea how he had muddled V's library. The texts and scrolls which Shilly had so carefully studied were now no more than randomly jumbled words which made no sense at all. Den comprehended the importance of keeping Bardook safe. He did not want V to ever have access to these secrets of the dark arts in the future. If they failed to defeat him he would surely use these spells and incantations to plan another threat. Bardook's safety ensured that V's access to the knowledge hidden in these texts would remain lost. Den charged Quays with Bardook's safety. Quay' Sea was the most powerful Society member to have come on this voyage and he would best stand a chance of keeping Bardook alive once V discovered that he had been betrayed.

Bardook and the Society members made their way hurriedly toward the main hall to meet Fannie and her companions. If any of them had known about V's stone of power which was buried deep beneath the spot where Manfred stood vigil, they could have ensured their victory before the battle even took place but fate was not with them on this occasion. They rushed right by the chamber, which housed and protected the stone, on their way to the stairways which would lead them up to the main hall.

The groups joined forces in the main hall and wasted no time before they began scribing their planned signatures into the granite of the floors. They used conjured acids which ate right into the rock so that signatures could not be changed or destroyed. They would serve to diminish V's powers and the intensity with which he could cast his spells. These symbols were discovered in V's own texts and re-created by Shilinar. Each member had memorized and practiced scribing a single signature so they could reproduce it easily. With the renderings complete, the infiltrators were ready to face V but they did not intend to face him inside his stronghold; they planned to lure him outdoors.

Fannie boldly threw open the main doors and let the wind blow wildly into the hall and up the stairway. The interlopers all made their way outside and stood in a single line facing the Enclave from a distance of 100 paces. Fannie sent her protected mind out to search for Vigour and announce her presence. She intruded while V was communicating with one of his followers in Kingsport. When he recognised Fannie, the look on V's face registered absolute incredulousness.

CHAPTER 42

THIS GIRL WAS bolder than V would have imagined. He would be pleased to welcome her back into his fold but he doubted that she was here to join him. He used his special connection to alert Bardook of the intruder who was outside the Enclave but he was surprised for the second time within moments. Bardook was outside the castle and he was in a group of people. Bardook did not have the power to keep V out of his mind completely. His ring connected him directly to his master and he did not possess the magic or the knowledge to remove the enchanted encumbrance. V looked through Bardook's eyes and became enraged with what he saw. The twins were both back and they had brought a troop of companions to threaten him in his own castle. Bardook had somehow found release from the library and he had joined the interlopers. Where were his children? V was becoming more perplexed and livid by the moment. Rather than react irrationally, V delayed and took stock of his situation. He would not be caught unawares again by the wily waif of a girl and her troublesome brother.

V unlocked and opened a silver box where he kept his special possessions. He slipped an object that looked like a large egg into one of the deep pockets of his flowing robe. He placed a ring on his left index finger which was dominated by a blood red stone the size of a sparrow's egg. Next, he removed a small satchel which was filled with a powdery substance finer than the sands of the Cordon Peninsula. He carefully opened the satchel and removed a pinch of the powder which he sprinkled over his head and body. V literally sparkled and reflected light where the powdery particles attached themselves to his body. He carefully re-sealed the satchel and placed it into another of his numerous pockets. Lastly, he removed a glove which had been tailored to fit his right hand like a second skin. The glove was woven through with threads of red, gold and silver which came together on the palm to form a spectacular glyph. Before V donned the glove, he laid it on the granite table and spoke several words of cogency which would assure that the glove obeyed the directions of the wearer. V forced his right hand into the glove and it sealed itself around his wrist where it melded with the skin of his arm. With his hair clasped firmly at the nape of his neck and held there with a charm decorated with a protective signature he turned to make his way to the main level to face his destiny. He would become the uncontested lord and master of all of Adnil after he destroyed the annoying Society members who dared confront him where he was most powerful. Den, Fannie and Bardook, the traitorous sot, would be saved so that V could punish them slowly as they rightly deserved. He would enjoy watching them suffer for a long while before he absorbed their life forces to feed his own insatiable hunger for power.

    V appeared calm and self assured as he stepped to the edge of the stairway which led down from the balcony, which fronted his Enclave. Den and Fannie stepped forward leaving their 18 members four paces behind them. They were not sure what to expect from V but they were already alarmed to find a composed and unruffled man who presented himself as unthreatened and confident as he faced 20 individuals who had come to force a standoff at his very doorstep. They had anticipated a surprised adversary who behaved irrationally and without focus. V gave off an iridescent glow as he stood silently sizing up the opposition. The conjured snowstorm was dwindling and V surveyed his rivals with serene satisfaction. He noted the sea vessel anchored not far off shore which was doubtlessly the conveyance used to arrive at North Point but V would be delighted to inform the throng he faced that they had journeyed for their last time. He chose not to address the shivering fools who had ventured this far just to die. Instead he slowly raised his gloved right hand, in what could have been mistaken as a gesture of welcome, and before anyone could react, long and jagged frozen bolts sailed from V's fingertips and skewered four of the members to the frozen ground where they stood. The victims had little time to register their fate before they froze into solid bloodied figures who would move no more.

    Fannie was horrified by the brutality she had just witnessed but she also sprung into action. She and Den both moved closer to their groups in an effort to protect them from further attack. They each created a shield of pulsing energy around their companions which would deflect further icy spears. Several of the members were already casting various spells meant to cause waves of heat to wash over Vigour. Fannie knew that heat was the one and only weakness that they had to exploit if they were to defeat this powerful sorcerer. V laughed out loud as the heat passed around him, reflected by the iridescent glow which surrounded him. Den spoke to Fannie in her mind;

they would have to think of something new to weaken V because he had obviously learned to protect his Achilles heel since they last confronted him. Planning on a battlefield was not the best circumstance. Fannie had been so sure that heat would weaken and ultimately destroy the evil lord of the north but she had underestimated his ingenuity. Now, because she had misjudged this worthy adversary, four Society members stood lifeless and frozen in their tracks and Fannie felt the responsibility for their gruesome deaths. Fannie's concentration wavered and her protective shield began to lose its viability.

V was powerful but he still remained human and he had to see his target before he could attack. Den took command and ordered all the members to run and seek cover. The crowd outside the Enclave dissolved into an undisciplined retreat which made V laugh even louder. With no defence barrier to protect them, several of the members were either severely injured or killed before they could find cover. Quay' Sea provided a secure refuge for himself and for Bardook as they huddled behind a large snowdrift around the side of the castle. Den and two other members ran into V's line of vision to move the injured members to a safe area. V was unconcerned and was rather enjoying toying with the annoying aggressors. Quay' Sea increased the size of his protective bubble to include the injured and Fannie who was doing her best to heal their wounds. Random members continued to barrage V with waves of heat and balls of flame. He remained untouched by their ever increasing efforts and actually appeared to enjoy the exercise. The members were incurring more injuries and without a backup plan, the battle seemed hopeless. Some of the members fled back to the place where they had stowed the dinghies in an attempt to get back to the ship. They were demoralized and drained from their futile attempts to weaken this supernaturally stalwart opponent. Those who ran for the beach were exterminated by a blast of icy power emanating from a red stone on V's left hand. V was absolutely giddy with excitement and he used his power to enhance and throw his voice so that everyone could clearly understand his words when he assured them all that they were about to die. Panic infected the membership and Fannie could feel their resolve dwindle and disappear as they quaked in their hiding places. So few were left alive and V enjoyed tormenting them as they lost all hope.

With their minds joined, Den and Fannie emerged from around the castle and faced V with a united front. He shifted his attention from the members who were left scattered and hiding behind the ice and snow. He glared at the twins as they approached the stairs that led to the castle's main hall. Den and Fannie stood ten paces apart and were enfolded in separate protective bubbles of vibrating colour. Fannie appeared green and Den looked violet as V studied his last somewhat worthy opponents. V was unable to read their thoughts because they had erected a barrier which kept them linked while keeping V completely blocked out.

Fannie's new plan did not include battling V personally but instead she counselled Den to aim all of his powers toward the Enclave itself. V was well protected and they had not had any success hurting him personally so they would try to hurt his habitat. While Fannie kept V's attention by using any spell she could imagine to break through his protective sheen, Den concentrated on conjuring a heated environment to encircle the castle. As soon as Den's spell began to warm the atmosphere around the bastion, V faltered and turned his interest toward the young man. Quay' Sea felt the temperature rise and cast a spell which caused the clouds to clear away and let the sunshine amplify Den's spell. The temperature continued to rise in and around the castle till it was absolutely tropical. The rock absorbed the heat quickly on the surface and while V was trying to deal with Den, some of the members sent heat into the castle in any form that they could conjure. The main doors still stood open and the hall was being filled with balls of fire and liquid fire. V's retreat had been cut off; he had no choice but to stand on the balcony and endeavour to protect his Enclave from the hot invasion. The liquid fire ran down stairways and caused the frozen rock to change temperature so quickly that minute cracks began to form. V ignored the twins completely as he cast spells to stop the fires which threatened his home. While V scrambled to cast spell after spell aimed inside his main hall, Den cast a melting spell which caused the base of the granite structure to heat up and bubble as it changed to its liquid state. The Enclave actually listed on its fluid foundation.

V would not lose his creation; his home. He howled with rage and turned on the twins with a look of pure hatred. He had protected himself but he had forgotten to ensure the environment of his power source. The stone was still safe, for the moment, but if the enchanted fires reached the chamber that protected his magical creation, the stone would crack and all would be lost. V stamped his foot and the fireballs ceased to burn. He pointed his gloved hand into the castle entrance and the liquid fire sputtered and fizzled out. The spell which was melting the very foundation had been cleverly cast and V would need time to counter it.

Fannie sent out a mental entreaty to the entire membership still hiding in the vicinity. They must continue their fire barrage to keep V occupied with multiple tasks so that he could not spare a moment to plan a counter attack. As the fire flew toward the castle, V erected a barrier across the doorway preventing any more damaging heat sources from entering. The fire no longer passed into the hall and V turned to face the twins.

Den and Fannie were steadfast as they slowly made their way toward each other in what would probably be their last stand. They were committed to defeating this sorcerer or die trying. As their protective bubbles came into contact they both reacted as one to the third voice in their joined minds. It was in this hour of dire need that the presence had chosen to make itself known. It spoke in a voice that was neither male nor female; and it counselled them to stand and face their destiny. The twins joined hands and locked their sights on V. They did not attempt to hurt him or cast spells against him. Instead they sent a beam which was a spiralling infusion of emerald green and violet, filled with the emotions of love, compassion and healing hope. The third presence added its power to the beam and it shot directly at V. The colours embraced V and cocooned him in an envelope of radiance. He stood, dumbfounded, with his arms loosely hanging by his sides. The glove he wore slowly disintegrated and the ring on his left hand shattered and the red crystals clattered onto the balcony. His iridescence ceased to glitter and the granite sparkles turned to dust and blew away in the light breeze. V's amber necklace cracked and fell at his feet and his hair clasp popped away and his hair sprang loose.

V stood shivering on the balcony of his castle with his scarred visage revealed for all to see. His bitterness had been washed away and with it his rage disappeared. Fannie and Den marvelled as the lonely and trembling man looked puzzled and disoriented. Tears were running down his disfigured face and he sank to his knees like a man without the strength to stand.

Fannie and Den approached the sorcerer with trepidation but were soon convinced that he was no longer a threat. They scanned his mind and determined that he was a gifted individual but he no longer emanated any hateful or evil thoughts. The main emotion in Vigour was a deep and sincere sadness. Den withdrew his spell so that the castle would not crumble and melt away into the ground. The cold quickly returned to the granite structure and although it had come dangerously close to being destroyed, the Enclave would settle and continue to stand on its hardening foundation. The remaining Society members, including Quay' Sea and the wounded, made their way to where Fannie and Den were helping Vigour to his feet and into the main hall.

They wrapped Vigour in a fur cloak which had been discarded on a large granite chair and led him into the mess. Den used his abilities to push together several chairs to form a makeshift fire pit. The members took turns keeping a fire burning in an effort to heat this room and keep it comfortable enough to speak with Vigour and try to unravel the puzzle of the effect their light beam had had on this snivelling man. Den and Fannie would explore the apparition which had made itself known to their minds at another time. First, they had to calm Vigour so that he could communicate rationally and possibly explain this bizarre circumstance.

Lucious and Kane made their way into the castle and laid the sleeping children close to the fire. When Vigour focused on the slumbering boys, he struggled in an effort to stand and go to them. Den convinced him to remain sitting until his strength returned and Fannie sent Vigour healing energy to speed his recovery. Evening was approaching and Vigour was finally strong enough to sit and speak with his guests. He spoke directly to Fannie; for some reason he had formed a personal bond with the raven haired girl.

CHAPTER 43

VIGOUR RAMBLED INCOHERENTLY for some time. Darina, wife, fire, death . . . Lily, the twins . . . Manfred . . . . Ben, Helga, Moira . . . . hate, power. He went on this way for some time and Fannie communed with Den before she took Vigour's hand and entered his mind to help him make sense of what he was trying to communicate. Fannie found no trace of the malevolence that she expected to encounter. A numbing sadness infected Fannie as she tried to lead Vigour's thoughts toward a rational recounting of what had led to his change of heart. She verbalized Vigour's thoughts so that everyone could hear and understand how they had come to be guests in the Enclave that they had come to destroy.

Fannie recounted Vigour's marriage to Darina, a beauty who had died in a fire while she carried her first child. She explained how Vigour had tried to save his love but he had chosen not to use his magic and he had been burned and almost drowned. His sensitivity to heat and his bitterness were all that were left to him after losing his Darina. He wandered the northern continent searching for redemption and a cool climate where he could experience relief from the pain he felt where the scars remained. At The Bay of Glaciers, Vigour had met Manfred who had recognised his gifts and had manipulated Vigour's bitterness into a hatred for all the citizens of Adnil. Together they plotted the destruction of The Society, a group of gifted people who were fostering the use of magic. Manfred had his own agenda which Vigour had never learned but Manfred did make a serious error by underestimating the power Vigour possessed. Once he had filled Vigour with hate and evil he schooled him in the use of the dark arts, and then was surprised one day when he inadvertently enraged his apprentice. Vigour's power had multiplied and when he unexpectedly turned on his mentor, Manfred was entirely unprepared. Vigour encapsulated his mentor in the statue which stood in the main hall. The lust for power was overwhelming and Vigour continued his mentor's plan to dominate the entire continent and rid the land of the hateful Society. He was fed by rage and struck out at those who angered or disappointed him. Lily was his wife and she stood as an effigy on the tower where her only transgression had been to beg for a chance to visit her parents. He had fathered two sets of twins with his lovely Lily. The boys were sleeping safely by the fire and the girls were hidden with their grandparents, Ben and Helga. Moira had become afraid during the battle on the beach but Vigour saw this as a betrayal and she suffered before he froze her in place in the stairway which led to the tower. He was also responsible for so many incidental deaths. Losing his original bitterness when he was enveloped by the lights conjured by Den and Fannie had melted away all of the evil which had been built on its firm foundation. Manfred was responsible for making Vigour into the evil sorcerer he had become but it was Vigour himself who would have to deal with the guilt he would carry for the deeds he had committed.

Vigour appeared to be a broken man but Fannie insisted that he could be rehabilitated and allowed to perform deeds that would make him proud to be a gifted sorcerer. Den suggested that Vigour should begin by freeing Lily and Moira from their marble prisons. It was late and everyone needed rest but when dawn brought the morning they would visit Lily's statue which now stood on the beach, facing the Bay of Ice. This would be the first night when Vigour would need heavy blankets to keep warm; he was no longer afflicted with pain when he was exposed to heat. Two members were assigned to watch Vigour as he slept. The children were wakened and fed and entrusted to the care of Bardook who knew them best. Den and Fannie sat together by the fire after everyone had retired. They agreed that the real evil in this Enclave was Manfred and they needed to consider how to deal with him. He was still alive and aware within his marble confinement but he couldn't be left with just this enchantment guarding him from escape. Perhaps Vigour would have a suggestion that would help Fannie and Den to feel more secure about Manfred's incarceration. Fannie was fatigued and Den was completely exhausted; first they would sleep and tomorrow they could plan their next course of action.

Fannie had forgotten how cold it was waking up in the Enclave. Den was asleep on the divan and was still securely wrapped in a large cover made of muskrat furs. Fannie gently nudged him with her mind and Den immediately responded. They woke the membership and everyone broke their fast compliments of Bardook who conjured warm bread and butter with a variety of cheeses, slices of fatty pork and platters of crunchy vegetables and delectable fruits. The hot chai was the best thing Den had ever tasted and he certainly appreciated the warmth which filled his belly. Vigour's twins sat close to their father and revelled in the attention for which they had yearned. Vigour smiled at his boys and sent them off to pester Bardook while he planned a family trip with Den and Fannie. The children were pleased with the notion of travelling with their father so they demonstrated an obedience which they had rarely displayed.

Quay'Sea joined the twins and they all sat around a granite table with the lord of this frozen bastion. Although Vigour had a lot to atone for, the twins assured him that he was not entirely responsible for the man he had been. Manfred had a personal vendetta against the Society and maybe Morgan would be able to shed some light on that situation when they spoke to him but in the meantime Vigour's cooperation and help were required. Quay'Sea volunteered his expertise to assist Vigour when he attempted to release Lily from her enchantment. Morgan and Quays had spoken at length about the spells which may release the trapped individuals but now that they had Vigour to do the casting, they were confident that Lily could be safely released.

Den led the way across the hard packed snow to the place where Lily's stature stood on the beach. Vigour was in a severely weakened state and he needed his power fortified by his three companions. Den and Fannie both laid a hand on each of Vigour's shoulders and Quay'Sea held Fannie's other hand. Through Fannie, the entire foursome linked and used their combined energy to cast Vigour's melting spell. Vigour held the palms of his hands aimed at Lily and they began to emanate a green flickering light. The shimmers coalesced and enshrouded the entire statue. The three members funnelled power into the spell through Vigour and Lily's encapsulating shell began to crack and crumble around her. The moments passed slowly and once Lily was almost completely free, she began to shiver and collapse. Fannie broke the connection and ran toward Lily to break her fall and to administer any type of healing that Lily may require.

Lily's life signs were weak and Fannie worked frantically to pump life energy into the near lifeless body which she held in her arms. Lily was beautiful and so delicate that Fannie believed that she could carry her without any help but as Quay'Sea assisted a weakened Vigour and Den scooped Lily up, the group rushed back toward the castle where they could warm and strengthen an unconscious Lily. Lily's fragile body was warmed by the fire in the mess and her eyes fluttered as she struggled to regain consciousness. Her twin sons' faces were the first images she comprehended as her tears of relief and appreciation rolled down her temples and into her hair. She lay on her back revelling in the sight of the children she had yearned to hold.

Vigour held her hand and when she turned to face him she shuddered and panicked. Fannie calmed her through her link and related all that had occurred including how Vigour had been cleansed of the bitterness and evil that had enchanted him and caused his malevolent behaviour. Lily stared into Vigour's eyes and recognised the man who had captured her heart while sitting on the stool in Big Ben's inn so long ago. His scarred face was full of remorse and regret as he wept silently over his wife. Lily embraced her children and held firm to Vigour's hand as she assimilated all the information which Fannie provided. Den signalled Fannie and they wandered to the other side of the room to give the newly reunited family some time to commune privately.

Quay'Sea and the royal twins were involved in an intense discussion regarding the possibilities for dealing with Manfred. Vigour approached the threesome and offered his counsel. Manfred had been and continued to be a very powerful sorcerer. If he had not been caught off guard, V would never have had the power to defeat his old mentor. The only way to ensure that Manfred remained imprisoned was to have several magicians or sorcerers cast numerous spells of confinement around the statue in the main hall. If anything were to happen to Vigour, his enchantments would fade and disappear over a short time and Manfred would find himself freed from the marble encasement. The other spells would serve to hold Manfred until a new encapsulation could be cast. Den summoned the Society members, and under the guidance of Quay'Sea, he charged them with casting a myriad of spells to guard against Manfred's escape. He and Fannie had business to conduct with Vigour in the tower's stairway.

Moira had been imprisoned for a relatively short time, her release was easier, and she maintained her strength as she was liberated from her bondage. Fannie linked with Moira and did for her all that she had done for Lily. She gave her energy and information. Moira was quick to understand her new circumstance and she was relieved by her new situation. She longed to be re-united with Lily and to atone for the atrocities she had endorsed. Moira was strong enough to descend the stairway with little assistance and she was grateful for the warmth provided by the fire in the mess.

Vigour spent the rest of the day and the evening communicating with his followers. Most of them were amenable to Vigour's new and unexpected instructions but a few were suspicious and puzzled by their master's new campaign. These few were individuals who had no spark of goodness in their hearts and would never be turned away from the dark arts; Vigour no longer held the same authority over them. They would be free to leave

Vigour's fold and do as they pleased although they would be forever joined to their old master through the ring which he had permanently attached to their fingers. Vigour bid the majority of his membership to make their way to the Isle of Solosk where they would meet with him. There was serious work to be done if they were to save Manek and all of Adnil from starvation and death.

Den and Fannie were distressed when Vigour admitted that he did not have a solution to defeat the spell he had loosed on Adnil. Moira knew the signatures that V had used and V knew the spell but he had not anticipated the need to ever counter the enchantment. V vowed to work ceaselessly with The Society to uncover a way to return the climate to its original state and to try to make amends for the travesty which was his doing.

They had done all that they could to fortify Manfred's imprisonment and they had cast spells of deflection around the Enclave to keep out the curious. The time had come to make their way back to Solosk where they could study and devise possible ways to correct the climate which threatened their collective homes.

CHAPTER 44

QUAY'SEA HELPED VIGOUR to carefully wrap and protect his stone of power. They moved it from its place in the centre of the protected chamber and packed it in a conjured crate where it would be protected during the journey. In its place, Vigour created a blue iridescent sphere which hovered in place and cast off the energy needed to keep the Enclave standing and the chamber impenetrable. Moira wanted to move the library in the centre of the labyrinth but Bardook assured her that it was of no use to anybody while his enchantment kept the writings jumbled and without coherence.

Lily wanted to delay their departure until her daughters could be fetched from The Bay of Glaciers but Vigour convinced her that they would remain safe in Ben and Helga's care. The shortages that were being experienced in the more populated parts of Adnil would not be felt any time soon in the north. There was good hunting and the fishers could provide sustenance if land animals became scarce. Lily was difficult to convince but she eventually accepted that the membership's first priority had to be accomplished so that everyone's security could be ensured.

Everybody bundled up and made their way to the dinghies which had to be magically released from the snow and ice which held them firmly frozen in place. Cresterman's sailors spotted the returning entourage and were ready to hoist them and the dinghies on board when they arrived. The General was relieved to see that Den and Fannie had persevered but he was saddened at the loss of many members who had given their lives to allow the battle to be won. The enchanted crate was stowed in a safe area and all of the members made their way to quarters where they could finally rest while the sailors hoisted the anchor and set sail for home. They were heading home victorious but bearing unfortunate tidings regarding the spell effecting Adnil. With Vigour's help, maybe Morgan would have a clue as to how to proceed.

The voyage became easier each successive day but the climate was clearly colder than it should have been as they sailed by the coast of Manek. The area was evidently in turmoil and a cloud of smoke hung over the city, probably caused by fires burning out of control. Morgan's prognostications had come to pass, after all. The shipyards were empty. All of the boats most probably had sailed south with passengers who could afford their doubtless pricey berths. The looting and thievery had begun and the survival of the fittest ruled Manek above all else. Vigour's regret was palpable as he gazed at the squalor that now existed where enterprise and order had ruled a short time ago. Quay'Sea journalized all that he witnessed as they slowly sailed by the ravaged city, which had been his home, so that he could later provide a detailed report for Queen Zelebeth, Prince Archer and Morgan upon his return.

The remainder of the journey passed without incident as the passengers revisited their personal visions and memories of a peaceful and vibrant Manek, ruled by Zelebeth and peopled with hardworking and loyal citizens. They were each willing to sacrifice whatever was necessary to ensure that the city once again returned to its past eminence. The rural citizens of Adnil may be faring with some success compared to the city dwellers. They had warning of this enchanted winter so they may have stored and preserved food to see them through this time of need. Without having witnessed it, Den and Fannie believed that the farmers were most likely defending their families and their dwindling food supplies from looters and gangs of marauders. An answer had to be discovered before it was too late to save the populace from degrading into hostile bands which chose violence and robbery above working toward the common good.

The armada that had been left to blockade Solosk from the mainland had been kept extremely occupied during the time it had taken to journey to and from North Point. General Cresterman's flag was spotted and he was welcomed by an exhausted fleet that sorely missed their captain. The sailors who had loyally protected the royal family on the isle of their self imposed exile had performed beyond the call of duty. The skirmishes with lesser vessels had been constant and came during daylight hours as well as in the dark of night. The people on the mainland were most certainly starving and they had persistently attempted to land on the island where they believed there was food to be had. Staving off the unrelenting attempts had taxed each and every sailor's stamina. The safe return of Cresterman and the Society members served to boost the spirits of the men and women who had given their all to follow the General's orders in his absence.

The Queen herself was on the dock to greet the returning journeymen. Their presence meant that they had succeeded and the Queen was most eager to hear good tidings from her siblings. Morgan stood at the Queen's side experiencing similar thoughts but he had sensed no readjustment in the climate patterns so he was reticent to appear celebratory before he was apprised of the situation.

After all the welcoming and relived hugs, Quay'Sea produced the list of the names of those who had not survived the journey. Zelebeth ordered a marble memorial stone to be carved with all the names of those brave souls who had valiantly given their lives in the service of Adnil. It had been hundreds of years since a memorial like this one had been necessary and no one alive had ever experienced a war-like battle.

Vigour, Lily and their twin sons were presented to the royal couple and Vigour not only swore allegiance but he begged forgiveness for his treacherous acts. Zelebeth was a magnanimous Queen and in her mercy, she granted that Vigour had been misled and was acting under an enchantment. Morgan was aghast when he heard that his old nemesis, Manfred, had been at the root of all the evil. All were dismayed when they learned that a counter spell to put right the climate of the continent was non-existent. Morgan assured the Queen that his members, with the assistance of Vigour and Moira, would apply themselves tirelessly to achieve a triumphant end to the looming threat. He could promise no more than his Society's continued efforts to untangle the enchantment which held the continent hostage. The Queen wanted to know more about Manfred and how Morgan had come to be his enemy.

Zelebeth was just a tiny princess when Manfred had come to Morgan and requested membership in The Society. Morgan had welcomed the new arrival and offered him all the comforts and privileges accorded to members. Manfred proved himself as a powerful and talented sorcerer. He had been schooled by witches and was comfortable wielding his powers and casting spells which were often tainted with the dark arts. Morgan had used diplomacy when he warned Manfred against the use of the dark arts but Manfred responded with obstinacy and arrogance. He felt that he was more powerful and therefore more experienced than Morgan. Ultimately, Manfred had initiated a coup in an effort to take over as chancellor of The Society. He had not bargained on the loyalty that Morgan engendered in his followers and was defeated when he challenged Morgan directly.

As punishment, Manfred's powers had been drained and he was turned out of The Society after his left hand had been branded to mark him as an undesirable individual. Vigour mentioned that he had never noticed a brand or marking of any kind on Manfred's hand. Morgan suggested that he may well have worn an amulet much like the amber charm that Vigour had worn to disguise his disfigurement. Vigour did recall Manfred wearing a leather thong bracelet with a silver charm with an embossed glyph. Manfred must have found someone who could serve as a channel for power which enabled him to regain the strength which The Society had drained. He had used Vigour as a pawn, nurturing his bitterness in an attempt to bring his own devious plot to fruition. Manfred's ultimate goal had been to destroy The Society which had shunned him and Morgan who had defeated and shamed him. If attaining his goal necessitated destroying an entire continent then he was satisfied to let that be so. If The Society were unable to find a way to alter the climate, Manfred may yet succeed in his original diabolical purpose.

By the time Morgan concluded his account, everyone was exhausted and in need of refreshment and sleep. Beginning the following day, each and every Society member planned to work diligently on developing a spell which would banish the continental threat once and for all.

CHAPTER 45

CRESTERMAN WAS GIVING orders to his fleet as dawn brightened the horizon; the blockade of Solosk must not be compromised. The safety of those who currently toiled to save Adnil from the creeping frost was of paramount concern. With their General back from his journey and at the wheel of his own sturdy ship, the sailors felt invigorated with new hope and fresh energy. With a restored motivation the sailors were eager to do their parts in this battle for the continent.

Den and Fannie met with Morgan privately to discuss the mystifying presence that had made itself known in their collective minds. They explained how the presence had guided their reactions to Vigour's assaults and had planted the spell they had cast into their arsenal of magic. Without the guidance of the peculiar mental apparition, the battle on the steps of the Enclave would most certainly have suffered defeat. The puzzling aspect of this benevolent entity was its ability to mask itself completely and make its presence known only when circumstances were dire. Den recalled feeling the entity when he and Fannie had joined together in an effort to save El after her agonizing labour. It manifested itself again during the battle with Vigour and on both occasions its energy flowed from the twins in the form of green and violet light. Both Fannie and Den sensed that the presence was never far from the surface in each of their minds but neither of them had been successful when attempting to communicate with it. Morgan suggested that the act of being in physical contact with each other may be the catalyst which springs the entity into action. During both occurrences when the presence had come forth to facilitate the outcome of a volatile situation, Den and Fannie had been not only mentally but physically connected. Morgan observed a mental picture in his mind when he heard a retelling and he often perceived the obvious which was not always apparent to the average person. This notion of physicality being the catalyst which allowed the presence to lend its guidance was certainly an avenue to study in the future. The twins intended to test Morgan's theory when an opportunity presented itself. In the meantime, they were dispatched to work with Shilly and Vigour who were accumulating possible avenues which could lead to the answer that, thus far, proved elusive.

The days passed monotonously as everybody on the island continued to hope and yearn for a breakthrough which would provide a clue as to where they should place their combined focus. The mainlanders had doubled their efforts to break the blockade and Cresterman was unsure how much longer the safety of the islanders could be maintained. The climate over the entire island had been manipulated by members assigned to the task and the cold was being held at bay. The farmers, like Jok, were harvesting the season's plantings to ensure a food source which did not have to be conjured. The gifted were too occupied with the current problem to warrant a waste of energy where it could be conserved. It was difficult to maintain a positive mood when all the efforts of the magicians were leading to one dead end after another.

Den and Fannie gazed dejectedly at Shilinar and Vigour across a table laden with scrolls and parchments. They were exhausted by all the castings they had undertaken over the last several months. Moira's fingers were raw from her design and creation of suggested amulets and signatures which were thought to be of importance. None of the spells had any lasting effect against the chill which promised to become a deep freeze before the turn of the next season. The royal triplets would be born on the only landform in Adnil still protected from the creeping winter.

Fannie attended her sister as soon as the first signs of labour presented themselves. Den made his way to the palace to ensure that Fannie would have support if the situation warranted their special intervention. As it happened, the Queen gave birth to her triplets without any magical intercession. Her labour was short and straightforward without complication or distress. Adnil was a continent which was transformed from an heirless land to one where three young princes stood in succession to the throne. Gaylord II, Apnee and Drysco were born in that order and they were each perfect yet different from each other. Gaylord II was fair and his face was wide and serene. Apnee was smaller and his complexion appeared snowy against his head of raven hair. Drysco, who was robust and vocal, resembled his father, Prince Archer. The island community would celebrate the successful births of the young additions to the Royal Family.

Fannie and Den infused Zelebeth with energy and a feeling of well being before they left Archer alone with his Queen and his newborn sons.

They would enjoy this special time of bonding before the infants were carried off by midwives to care for their needs. Three was a number which brought good fortune and Den perceived the straightforward births as a good omen. Fannie's spirits were also high as she and Den made their way back to Shilinar's chambers to resume their labours.

Vigour was puzzled and becoming excited as he watched Shilinar B'Edard scurry around the chamber wringing his hands and pausing occasionally to slap himself across his own forehead. Shilly had realized that the spells they had been casting to stop the menacing cold were absolutely extraneous. He hypothesized that the same spell needed to be recast but in its opposite form. How this puzzle had eluded him for such a long time when the answer now seemed so blatantly obvious was mind boggling. Fannie linked with Shilly to help him calm himself so that he could apply his new idea within an ambience of tranquility. His demeanour settled into a mode of complete concentration and organization. He bid Vigour to search for the original scrap where the spell was scribed. The stone of power which had remained packed in its crate had to be uncovered, inverted and activated to produce the opposite form of energy but the same conditions which existed at North Point the day that Vigour had performed the dreadful casting. Moira was put to work recreating mirror images of the signatures and glyphs which had magnified Vigour's powers on the castle tower. Mushookoalah occupied himself by searching out and delivering the items Moira needed to reproduce her artistic renderings. Den estimated that they would be prepared within the next few days to attempt this desperate endeavour to reign victorious over the all encompassing winter.

The Queen opened her treasury where Mushy collected gold, silver and even copper which Moira required. The tanners provided various acids and chemicals, which they used in their trade, for Moira's magical purposes. Mushy collected special sands and salts which were necessary to produce specific signatures. Moira meticulously recreated the mirror images of each design she had furnished for Vigour on the platform located on the highest tower of the castle at Solosk. Mushy began to feel personally responsible for the wear treads on the staircase leading up to that tower.

Shilly scribed the original spell in its backward order and Vigour had practiced the foreign sounding words until he was able to recite them in his sleep. His stone of power was inverted and placed in the spacious portico leading to the tower entrance. Morgan and Quay'Sea supervised every detail of the preparation for this endeavour. The twins would support

Vigour by infusing as much power as they could into his enchantment as he released his counter-spell toward the north. Everyone had their assignments for the following day when The Society would either fail or finally taste victory.

CHAPTER 46

VIGOUR TOOK DEN aside on the morning of the planned casting. He was well prepared and optimistic about the outcome of the spell he would soon release. Den watched as Vigour reached into one of his deep pockets and produced a large smooth rock shaped like the egg of some giant bird. It was grey and unspectacular until one looked at it closely. It was covered with a minuscule veined design which sparkled with a vibrant intensity. Vigour placed the stone into Den's hands and he was surprised at its insignificant weight. He held it reverently as Vigour confided that he was entrusting his most precious belonging into Den's care. If the spell should somehow go awry, Vigour wanted Fannie and Den to keep and protect this treasured object. Vigour had been funnelling energy into the item ever since he had removed it from the enchanted box where he had stored it back at his Enclave. The energy was vital and Vigour had Den vow to continue feeding energy into the stone while it was in his possession. Vigour was unwilling to share more information so Den agreed to do as he was bid. When he was alone, Den attempted to probe the stone with his gifts but all his magic was deflected by the scintillating veins. His concerns were not imperative so he remained satisfied to hold Vigour's treasure until he could give it back.

Every detail of this auspicious undertaking had been checked and re-checked until everyone agreed that the time had come to let fate take its course. Vigour and Moira positioned themselves on the tower where Vigour stepped lightly between the signatures to his casting location. His powers were brimming and Moira stood by to assist Vigour if he should falter. The stone was in place below in its inverted position and the membership was lining the castle walls from where they could witness the entire undertaking. Morgan and Quay'Sea stood anxiously hopeful along with Zelebeth and Archer. Cresterman had sailed his fleet into close proximity of the castle so that he and his men could watch the spectacle from across the waters.

It was ironic that all their hopes now lay with the very individual who had been responsible for the original curse that afflicted their continent.

Vigour intended to succeed because he now owed his life to The Society, which he had once hated and plotted to destroy.

Vigour gathered his power and held out his arms in the same positions where he had held them on his icy tower several seasons ago. He glanced at Moira who was nodding her approval and he began reciting the spell in its reversed order. Orange vibrating rings of energy left his fingers and made their way north and a red luminescence ran down his body and over the signatures to finally drip off the tower's edge. The red sparkles disappeared into the ground and Cresterman would later report that he and his crews were astonished as swarms of red flashes, which appeared as schools of fish, swam by his vessels heading in a northern direction. V remained standing, holding his position and his concentration for as long as his body allowed. When he finally collapsed, drained of all his energy, he smiled because he was convinced that the spell had done his bidding. There had been no distraction, this time, to impede the casting and Vigour expected favourable changes in the climate to manifest themselves rapidly.

Lily's tears of relief were streaming down her face because she had been present and aware when Vigour had unleashed his original spell and she recognised the signs of the success of this new casting. They would not be sure if the spell had worked until they saw the physical evidence of warming on the mainland but this day's efforts were cause enough to celebrate. Meat would be roasted and music would be ordered. Mead and brew would flow freely as the loyal subjects on the island came together to celebrate fate's turn of events.

Den reached for Fannie's hand and when they touched, a voice inside both their heads shouted . . . . BREAK THE EGG. Without releasing his hold on Fannie, Den reached into his cloak and produced the stone which belonged to Vigour. The egg sparkled brilliantly in the sunlight and was encapsulated with green and violet shimmers. Somehow the egg was draining power but not from Den or Fannie; it was being fed by their secretive presence. The egg began to exude heat and Den was no longer able to keep hold of it. The episode was gathering attention from the crowd and Quay'Sea and Morgan rushed to where the twins were standing with the enveloped stone. They all watched as the egg fell from Den's hand and burst on the castle walkway. The shell lost its luminescence as it shattered and two tiny beings were left on the parapet staring up at Den and Fannie. The twins stooped to study the tiny lizard like animals which immediately jumped onto each of their shoulders. The twins were linked so, as one, they recognized that these were baby dragons. The newly hatched beings were linked into the twin's minds and they were bonding themselves to their new masters. Zosha was almost completely white, except for a red streak at her neck. She spoke to Den and Draken addressed Fannie. Draken was crimson with a slash of white at his neck. All the communication happened in their minds so the witnesses heard nothing of the secret communion. These dragons possessed all the memories and knowledge that Den and Fannie held. They were like magical children who knew their parents' every thought, dream and memory. The dragons were twins and they were meant to be paired with twins. Fannie and Den both sensed that this was the beginning of a long and binding relationship. Den hoped that Vigour would understand that he had not chosen to bring life to these beautiful dragons. They had chosen the moment of their arrival. The voice which had encouraged Den to break the egg had once again grown distant and silent. They would not find any answers to their questions from the taciturn mentor in their minds.

Morgan was both aghast and delighted by the birth of the dragons. He had studied the lore which he had been able to gather and was quite the expert when it came to the care and feeding of these tiny yet fierce creatures. The pair was spectacular; mirror images of each other in colour. Draken was slightly larger but Zosha had a more exquisite visage. They needed constant attention and their bonded masters were the only ones who could provide for their needs. Dragons were slow to develop trust with humans and they refused to be handled by anyone but Fannie and Den. Vigour was impressed and a little envious of the twins' ability to hatch the twin dragons because he had tried countless times to urge their birth. He concluded that the dragons had chosen their masters and he did not aspire to stand in the way of that choice. Den and Fannie found themselves as willing and excited nurturers for the newest members of The Society.

Before the moon had completed five full cycles, Cresterman's ships were approached by small fishing vessels which carried news of spring on the continent. The orchards which had managed to survive were flowering in anticipation of a crop which had been sorely missed. The frozen edges of the creeks and lakes were thawed and once again supporting life. The people of the continent had been tested by the lurking evil but spring brought renewed hope and an opportunity for everybody to repent and return to the lives which they had been denied. Much hard work lay ahead for the citizens of Adnil because their continent had to be nurtured back to life so that it could once again produce the life sustaining crops that would feed its populace.

Magic had reared its dark side and threatened their lives but magic had also cured the land of the horrible curse. Many would remain superstitious but many others would become more accepting of what the gifted had to offer. If the citizens refused to support those who had risked all to save Adnil, where would they find themselves if another menace threatened their way of life? Morgan was confident that he and his royal benefactors would meet with less resistance when they advocated The Society in Manek.

Within the year, Zelebeth planned to return and take her throne in her palace in Manek. The true account of what had occurred was scribed and magically reproduced so that the tale could be carried by messengers, far and wide and shared with the ordinary citizens. The Queen firmly believed that her subjects had the right to know how they had narrowly escaped with their continent intact, thanks to the diligent efforts of The Society. The Queen implored her loyal subjects to make their way back to their towns and farms where they could resume the peaceful lives to which they had been accustomed. She promised that before her children took their first steps, she would be in Manek, ruling as she always believed her father had intended.

Peace and order returned slowly to the continent. The upheaval took time to fade and the enterprise in Manek was just beginning to return to normal when the Royal Family and their Society sailed back to the docks from which they had fled. The citizens were in a festive mood as they lined the coastline to extend a welcome home with the pageantry, the pomp and the circumstance essential for an event of such great magnitude.

The End

THE CHARACTERS:

IN ORDER OF APPEARANCE

Fannie and Den	the twins of Crerar
Fiona	The twins' adoptive mother
Lars	The twins' adoptive father
Marva	Mute and almost blind woman Midwife's assistant
Martine	The main elder of Crerar
Jok	A farmer in Adnak
Patrice	Jok's late wife
El	Jok's second wife (deaf and mute)
Frederer Senior	El's brother
Mica	Jok and El's first son
Nina	Jok and El's daughter
Frederer	Jok and El's second son
Edna	El's midwife
Carlotta	Society investigator
Eudora	Society elder (Carlotta's aunt)
Queen Zelebeth	Ruling sovereign of Adnil
Prince Archer	Zelebeth's husband
King Gaylord	Zelebeth's late father
Queen D'Enfanel	Zelebeth's mother
Mango	Manek fruit vendor
Archel	Society member
Morgan Alfred-son	Society chancellor
Carl	Dark magician and spy
Vigour "V"	Most powerful dark arts sorcerer
Darina	V's first wife
Lily	V's second wife
Moira	V's soul mate and concubine
Big Ben	Lily's father and pub owner
Helga	Big Ben's wife, Lily's mother

Manfred	V's mentor, dark arts practitioner
Kern and Zephyr	V and Lily's twin boys
Shandra and Frosh	V and Lily's twin girls
Shilinar B'Edard	"Shilly" Fannie's friend at the Enclave from Locan
Mushookoalah	"Mushy" Fannie's friend at The Enclave from Yama, in the open territory
Molisana	Enclave chess champion
Bardook	Fannie's tutor at the Enclave
Bin	Candidate—gifted to follow spells
Churl	Candidate—gifted to follow spells
Vlad	Captain of a northern fishing trawler
General Cresterman	Captain of ship, Morgan's friend
Lucious	Society member
Kane	Society member
Gaylord II	Oldest royal triplet, born on Solosk
Apnee	Middle royal triplet, born on Solosk
Drysco	Youngest royal triplet, born on Solosk
Zosha	Female dragon; connected to Den
Draken	Male dragon; connected to Fannie

The Lands of Ahul

Adnil "The northern continent"

Adnak: Capital-Manek
Afshen
Kandar: Capital: Lozka
Kazmeel: Capital: Lochko
Land of the White Bear
Locan N.: Capital: Kingsport
Madyar: Capital: Port of Merle
Midnight Territories
Prain Territory
Snowfell
The Waste

Shangie "The southern continent"

The Barrens
B'Endar: Capital: B'Ashir
Blaze Arm: Capital: Eva
Blue Coast: Capital: Bibo
Caravette: Capital: Bobek
Cordon Peninsula
Cormer: Capital: Janine
Crerar: Capital: Mantee
Crescent Islands
Darmor: Capital: Elda
Djingar Province
Gulya: Capital: Noha
Juanta: Capital: Lesha
Koshek: Capital: Sandel
Land's End Island
Locan S.: Capital: Lispur
Sonda: Capital: Oozo

Goji "The desert continent"

Unexplored

Edwards Brothers,Inc!
Thorofare, NJ 08086
06 December, 2010
BA2010340